The Reluctant Pirate

John Guy

First published on Kindle in 2013 by John Guy

ISBN-13: 978-1494886691

ISBN-10: 1494886693

Disclaimer. This is a work of fiction. All the characters are purely imaginary and any resemblance to any actual person is coincidental and unintended.

DEDICATION

For Louise

CHAPTER ONE

The grizzled old Yemeni dhow master felt his hand shaking. He was not used to feeling scared. Thirty years working the Arabian coasts had made him hard. His tough little ship looked after his cargoes. His old Kalashnikov looked after his ship. But this was different. Dealing with Yusuf Sugulle was never easy.

"*Asalamalakum,*" he said politely, keeping his eyes on the short balding man in front of him. "I bring greetings and a personal message from Ah Hing."

He hesitated. It was not easy to threaten a Somali pirate leader. Especially when you are standing right in front of him on his own beach.

"Ah Hing sends you this cargo and wishes you good hunting," continued the master. "Good, profitable hunting." He swung his arm, taking in the new wooden skiffs, drums of fuel and brand new Yamaha 60 hp outboard motors being unloaded from the dhow onto the beach behind them.

"Ah Hing asked me to tell you personally that you have all that you need now," he went on. "He said I should make sure you understand that he is eagerly awaiting a return on his investment."

The dhow master waited for a reply. He could see the rage in the man's eyes, but he did not turn away.

"Tell Ah Hing the monsoon will change now, and he will be paid. He will be paid handsomely," said Yusuf. The master could see one gold tooth glinting as Yusuf spoke. He had to lean forwards slightly to hear the last part of the reply. "And take care, old man, who you carry such messages to."

* * *

Abdi thought they could do with a bit of rain around here. They could do with some decent roads. The Land Cruiser was bashing through the scrub beside the track, which was full of huge potholes. He swayed against the young Somali guy on his left, who did not move. Could do with a shower too, thought Abdi. What the hell was his name?

They had been in the Toyota for five hours already. The driver and one old guy in the front, two younger guys either side of Abdi in the back. I'm the only one without a gun, thought Abdi. They had told him their names when they had picked him up on the tarmac at Mogadishu airport. He had forgotten them in the confusion. He hadn't expected to see men with guns meeting him from the Jubba Airlines plane from Dubai. Hadn't expected to see dollars changing hands to the fat bloke in the Customs shed. Hadn't expected to be pushed quickly into the back of a jeep. Don't get so many Toyotas in Butetown, he thought.

Somalia doesn't look too lush, he said to himself. They had passed a few small towns of low-rise buildings, goats and children wandering around. The countryside was flat, dry and boring. Abdi was a city boy. Born and brought up in Cardiff. He had never been abroad until now. The Cardiff Bay High School he had just left didn't do school trips. Or Muslim boys didn't do school trips, thought Abdi. Too busy helping our fathers. And our cousins.

Abdi tried to talk to the boy on his right. "How long till Harardhere?" he asked. He spoke Somali at home and used that now. On Saturdays he spoke Somali when he served the Butetown housewives their goat meat. He worked in his cousin's halal butcher in the Bute Street parade. His Somali didn't work here. No-one replied.

The jeep crashed to a halt beside what Abdi thought was a half-built breeze block garage. The driver turned to look at him. "Eat now," he said in slow, clear Somali, miming putting food in his mouth. "This restaurant. You no speak here. Only eat. No good place for Engelish boy. More five hours road after. Then coming your wife." Abdi caught the word wife. The others were all laughing at him. He thought he had made a big mistake to come to Somalia.

* * *

MT Prometheus wasn't quite what Lisa was expecting. This was her first trip as a second mate after getting her watchkeeping certificate. All the ships she had trained on had been Norwegian-owned. Clean, modern ships. The *Prometheus* was neither.

She felt herself sweating slightly. The air conditioning was struggling in the heat where the ship lay alongside the oil loading terminal in Fujairah. Had she done the right thing? To trust a Greek shipowner? For her first voyage as an officer? She shook herself slightly and straightened her back. She needed a job, and there were no jobs on Norwegian ships for newly-qualified officers. The shipping market was terrible and Norwegian owners were cutting back. Her new employer, CanDoTank, was owned by John Canopoulos, son of one of the big names of Greek shipping. He was well known as a businessman and had a high profile. His ships must be well run, she thought.

She put down her case and handed her seaman's book and certificate of competency to the grey-haired Greek captain. He flipped through the seaman's book, looking at the names of her previous vessels. "Welcome, Miss Aarberg," he said, looking up with a slight smile at the short, wiry young woman facing him. "You are welcome. This is not such a smart ship as some you have sailed on, and not so very big, as you see. But we are making money for the owner and in this market we can be glad of that. The mate you are relieving had to go already for the plane, so let me show you the ship. Then you can talk with the chief mate about duties."

Courteously the captain ushered her out of his dayroom and up the stairs to the small bridge. "She was built in Turkey in 1992," she heard as they looked forward through the bridge windows at the cargo deck. "We can carry 5,500 tonnes of oil in twelve tanks, and right now we are loading diesel fuel for East Africa. You make us a little more international even. The chief mate, Andrei, is Romanian, most of the engineers are from Poland and the cook and sailors from Croatia, and I am from the island of Skopelos. The same island as Mr Canopoulos. Or I should say, as the father of Mr Canopoulos, I am from the same village."

Lisa looked up from the rusting deck below and smiled at the captain. "Thank you," she said. "I thought I would be sailing now on a Bergesen VLCC. This will be different, but I am here to work and glad for the opportunity. Canopoulos should be a good owner to sail for." She was not sure if she meant what she said, but she saw that she had said the right thing.

The ship might be old and tired, but she needed a job. The Scottish manning agency that placed a global market of seafarers into a global market of shipowners and managers had assured her this was a good company. The captain was obviously proud of his links with the owner. She would make it work. It was only for three months, and then perhaps the market would change and Norwegian owners would be hiring again.

* * *

Yusuf was proud of his Ristorante. There was nothing else like it in Harardhere. He had built it in 2006 when forcing foreign fishing boats working off the coast of Somalia to pay a fat fee was both patriotic and personally profitable. The brightly-painted rendered breeze block walls and tin roof housed a large room where all the powerful men in the locality had come to eat and chew quat. And sometimes to drink.

Today there was no alcohol on the table. And no quat. The four men sitting opposite Yusuf had taken his hospitality in the past. Today they would take only water. He listened to them now. They would not have spoken to him this way last year. When his boats and his boys were going out from the coast and bringing back merchant ships and fishing boats to the Harardhere anchorage. There was none of this talk when planes were dropping millions of dollars in ransom payments every month.

Then there had been cash for everyone. Then they had called him the Guardian of the Seas. Then they said he looked after Somalia's coast and waters. They had been glad to come to his restaurant. Glad to chew the tender quat flown in from Kenya daily. Glad to drink Black Label whisky with him. Glad to take the envelopes of cash home in their new Toyotas.

Yusuf spat on the floor. He had heard enough. Enough from these tribal elders. Enough from the self-elected Minister of Fisheries for the self-administered autonomous State of Galmudug, or Somalia, or who knows where, thought Yusuf. Enough of how he was bringing disrepute on Somalia, affecting foreign aid. Enough of how local boys were dying because the weather had turned when it should not have. Enough of how Somalia now had a new and official Coastguard. Enough of hypocrisy.

"You are right," he said, palms held forward. "You are right. We must obey the law and protect our clan. But we must also protect our coasts. We must not allow fish to be stolen. We must not allow waste to be dumped off our coasts. We must be strong and families must fight together so that Al Shabab does not turn our boys into madmen."

Yusuf stood and escorted the men to the door. His words were empty. They knew that. Yusuf knew they knew. It was simply a warning. It was time for success. Time to bring in some big money. There was no place in Somalia for a failed pirate leader.

.

CHAPTER TWO

Yusuf held his arms open. He looked up at the tall boy who unwound himself from the Toyota. He stepped forward and held him in a hug.

"Welcome, my son," he said. "You are welcome in my house, the best house in Harardhere. I have lived a long time for this day. Ahmed's son is my son and soon you will marry my daughter. This is your house now."

He released Abdi and waved away the driver and guards. He led him across the walled-in courtyard and into the two-storey breeze block house.

"Soon you will meet Amina. This is a modern house, just like you have in Cardiff. We can talk with our women. You will see what a bride you will have. But first a drink and we talk. We don't need women for that," said Yusuf, laughing as he snapped his fingers at a servant girl.

"Bring whisky. Bring quat. Bring water," he ordered.

Abdi looked at the bright cushions beside the low dark wood table. The room was cool and dim. He did not know what to expect. He was surprised to see a TV set to one side and a laptop on a table. He could hear the hum of a generator. He thought it was better than he had expected.

"I bring greetings and respect from my father," he said politely to Yusuf. "He often talks about you. He says you are a powerful man. He told us how you and the clan helped him and my mother escape the war in Somalia. He has always told me that when Amina came of age I would marry her. It is an honour for me to come here."

Abdi was not sure he meant an honour, but the occasion seemed to call for a formal speech. He saw Yusuf pouring Black Label whisky into tumblers. Abdi had never drunk whisky. At home he hardly drank alcohol. He wanted to be fit for football. And drinking cost money. He wanted to save his.

Yusuf handed Abdi the glass of whisky.

"Perhaps in Cardiff you have better whisky," he said. "Here in our humble house it is the best we have."

He watched Abdi sniff the drink and sip it. He thought this was not a boy who drank. Good for Amina, he thought. But now he will drink, and listen.

Yusuf pushed the bundle of green quat towards Abdi and pulled some leaves and twigs out for himself.

"We take quat, we drink, you will tell me how is your life in Cardiff," he ordered.

* * *

Abdi was tired from the journey. He thought that Yusuf did not mean he wanted to hear about Cardiff. He had not asked about Abdi's life. He had not asked about Ahmed or his mother. He had not asked how their clan survived in the Somali community in Cardiff.

Yusuf slumped on the cushions. The pile of chewed quat leaves beside him was growing. The level of whisky in the bottle went down. He was talking more urgently now.

Abdi heard how he was a clan leader. How the Sacad-Hawiye clan ran Harardhere. How Yusuf was a coastguard. How he protected the Somali coast by forcing foreign fishing boats to pay to fish. How foreign ships dumped toxic waste in Somali waters. How Yusuf and his boys made the ships pay.

Under Yusuf's glare Abdi had drunk some whisky and taken a mouthful of quat leaves to chew. At home only losers chewed quat. Only losers drank. He hated feeling out of control.

As Yusuf rambled on Abdi thought Yusuf too was a loser. Through the fog of the whisky and quat he heard Yusuf. He was complaining now. Ahmed had taken the money and had a good life in the safety of the West. Yusuf had stayed in Somalia. He had fought for his clan. Ahmed made easy money driving a nice taxi. Yusuf had made money by taking ships. It was not easy money. Ahmed had a fine son. Allah had given him only four daughters. Ahmed was safe. Here the ships shot back. Ahmed could worship at the mosque. Yusuf had always praised Allah but the Islamists attacked his coastguard and stopped it working. Now the monsoon was blowing when it should not, so his boats could not work. Now the foreign navies stopped his boys and took their guns and boats.

Abdi had no need to reply. No need to drink. He sat quietly as Yusuf droned on. Abdi could only just understand. He spoke Somali at home but English in the street and at school. The Somali he was used to hearing was lifted by Welsh words and accents. He understood Yusuf was not happy. That his investors were pushing him. That the local elders were pushing him. That it was hard to get money to buy boats and weapons and fuel. Hard to keep up a house full of women.

A loser and a pirate. My father in law, thought Abdi. What have I let myself in for?

* * *

The recoil slammed the Kalashnikov into Abdi's shoulder. He winced. The gunfire had deafened him. He shook his head to clear it. He had hardly drunk whisky the day before but he felt muzzy and slow in the hot sun.

"You grow up soft in Cardiff," shouted Yusuf. "Here our boys grow up with guns. Take aim, hold the gun down, fire again. Two bullets only each time." He was pointing at an old drum fifty yards away. Abdi knew he had missed it with his first shots. The burst of gunfire had pushed the rifle skyward, sending the bullets into the red sand cliff.

They were on the beach. Abdi knew Yusuf was testing him. They had stripped the Kalashnikov and reassembled it. Yusuf had showed him the simple parts. Now he had to control the gun. "The boys here are stupid, they fire the gun with one hand, into the air, anywhere," said Yusuf. "You are a clever boy. In Cardiff they teach you. Here I teach you. Learn to use the gun. Learn to hit the target. You have to carry every bullet. Make every bullet work."

Abdi braced himself and pulled the gun into his bruised shoulder. He would not show that it hurt. If this loser could shoot then he would learn to shoot better.

When Abdi could hit the drum and keep the bursts of gunfire to two or three rounds each, Yusuf took the rifle. He put it into the back of the old jeep they had driven down from the village and reached under a pile of rags.

He was laughing at Abdi's face. "You think you know

the gun now, my son," he said. "This is another thing. With this you can destroy a boat or a jeep."

Abdi eyed the Rocket Propelled Grenade launcher. He had seen RPGs in pictures. But when his father told him it was his duty to come to Somali and marry Amina, he had not expected that using one would also be a duty.

Yusuf showed Abdi how to insert the charge and pre-warm the weapon. "You get only one chance with this," he said. He was leering at Abdi. "If you miss, then the people you shot at will kill you. There is no time to reload. So don't miss. Amina would not be happy to lose her husband before she has enjoyed her first night."

CHAPTER THREE

She has got a great figure, thought Abdi. She was covered from neck to toe in a long gown but Abdi thought it showed as much as it hid. He was trying not to stare at Amina. He could see she was trying not to stare at him. He didn't know what to say.

He thought of his sisters. They would tease him if they saw him now. They teased him when they caught him looking at their friends. "I have sisters," he said suddenly. "Like you." He felt suddenly foolish. Why did he say that? He was homesick. Last week he had finished his A-Level exams. The highest school exams he could sit in Wales. He had left school. He hoped to go to Cardiff University. He wanted to be an optometrist. Work in a nice clean shop, selling glasses. So why was he sitting in a house in Somalia? Why was he going to marry the daughter of a pirate?

"I will like to meet your sisters," said Amina, in English. She spoke very quietly, looking down at the floor. "I will like to go to Cardeef. With you." She wore a scarf covering her head, but Abdi had seen her small, sharply planed face and big eyes.

She had a soft, husky voice. Abdi felt his stomach turn over. He knew what some of the boys shouted at the girls at school. He had heard his mates boasting about the kaffir girls they had shagged. The fat white girls from Grangetown. Showing all their legs. Those slags. He had nothing to say to them. Now he had nothing to say to his wife. The girl he had promised to marry.

Beside him a servant girl knelt and placed a cold drink on the low table. From the tray she took a bowl of cashew nuts to place neatly with the drink. Abdi almost laughed. The sons of Cardiff Somali taxi drivers don't get waited on, he thought. Maybe this won't be such a bad move after all.

* * *

Yusuf thought his wife was a good woman. A quiet and virtuous woman. She wore the burqa. She cooked good goat risotto. In the dark of their room she did not refuse him.

He thought she had changed. The wedding plan had made her into a new woman. He did not know peace in his own house. Every day she had questions. Their daughters had questions. Amina had the most questions. All the questions had only one answer. Money.

When would the *Nikah*, the tying of the knot, be held? *Inshallah* when the monsoon changes and we have another ship ransom. When could they begin to invite all the relatives and clan to the wedding party? *Inshallah* when the monsoon changes. When could they buy their new *diracs*, the flowing gowns they must have for such an important wedding? *Inshallah* when we get paid next. How much money would he give out to each relative at the wedding? The *sooryo* must be at least twenty dollars for each guest or they would be shamed. *Inshallah* it would be more than twenty dollars, his daughter would not be shamed.

When? – "Enough," shouted Yusuf. "Enough. Use the internet. Buy the clothes you want. I will get money. I will get a ship. I have said Amina will marry Abdi and she will. No-one will ever forget their *Nikah*. But first Abdi comes with me to take a ship. Then we fix a date. Then you call your cousins and their cousins and half of Cardiff and half of all Somalia can come here for the wedding party. Now go and cook."

* * *

Ah Hing was flexing his arm muscles. He watched the tattoos ripple when he squeezed his fists. His face was immobile. He was listening to the phone on loudspeaker. Through the floor to ceiling apartment window in front of him he could see the Dubai beach stretching away into the distance. He did not look behind. He knew what was there. Two young Thai girls were standing there. It was time for his massage. They would be very young, he thought, but very strong.

He spoke sharply, loudly, cutting off the words coming from the loudspeaker. "Mr Sugulle," he hissed. "You got my cargo. You got my message. My dhow captain has told me that you look healthy. But you are still on shore. My investment is in ship hijacking. Not in sitting at home with the women drinking whisky."

He stopped talking. He would let the fool Somali talk some more. Then he would make him understand he could not take an investment from a Chinese Malaysian triad and not deliver. He wanted another successful hijack. It was good business. Safer than people smuggling. No trace back to him, and no threat of the death penalty for drug trafficking into this benighted Arab country. A few thousand dollars to buy boats and weapons, the fool Somalis risked their lives and he got paid fifty times over. No risk to him and his dhows that took the boats and engines and fuel and weapons into

Somalia and Yemen and brought back lucrative cargoes of charcoal for the Dubai shisha cafes.

Ah Hing turned his chair slowly to look behind him. Yes, he thought. My people have chosen these girls well. He thought his network had only brought them to Dubai that week. Fresh, he thought. They will look after me now. Then they will be put to work to make money for me.

"Mr Sugulle," he shouted, stopping the flow of Yusuf's justifications and demands. "There is no more money from me. Go to sea. There are no ships where you are now. Go to sea, capture a ship, get the ransom, then pay me. My reach is long, and my eyes are sharp. When you are at sea your wife and daughters will be safe. I will make sure of that. But if you do not pay me and pay me well, they will be the first to pay. There will not be enough guns even in Somalia to keep them safe if you do not pay me."

He reached across the glass desk and snapped the phone off. He sat still for a moment. Behind him he heard one girl draw in her breath. He almost smiled. You can be scared, he thought. He stood up slowly and undid his silk gown.

* * *

Yusuf was speaking quickly into his mobile phone. The line to Mogadishu was never up for long.

"Yes," he told his clan cousin. "Yes of course I have an investor. I will be able to pay. You must be patient. When have I not paid before? You have grown rich from me."

Yusuf hated to beg. He needed a delivery of Kalashnikovs, at least two more RPGs and plenty of ammunition. His cousin was close to the market in Mogadishu. Every weapon could be had there. But credit for pirates cost one hundred per cent, and he thought that credit for pirates who had not had a recent success was going to be set even higher.

Yusuf did not need the weapons to capture the ship. He would need them once the ship was taken. In Somalia the strong feed on the weak. When he brought a hijacked ship to anchor off Harardhere it was worth millions of dollars. That was when he needed a good squad of boys with plenty of weapons to keep the ship safe from other clans until the ransom came. He grinned suddenly as he thought. He would need the guns to protect his village when he had millions of dollars again, and was spending a lot of them on his daughter's wedding.

"Cousin," he said, firmly. "I am sending two jeeps tomorrow. Have what I ask ready. You will be paid and paid well." He cut the line.

CHAPTER FOUR

John Canopoulos did not like talking with his captain. There was nothing he could put his finger on. He felt the captain did not give him the respect he gave to his father. And in his experience captains only called the owner when they wanted something expensive.

He squeezed his stomach in a little and sat more upright in the seat of his Range Rover. He was sure that girl in the red car had recognised him. He thought she would be happy tonight, telling her friends she had been next to John Canopoulos in a traffic queue.

The captain's voice was distorted. He was calling John C's mobile over a satellite phone. John C was right. The captain was worried about security and obviously wanted to spend some money. Money John C did not want to spend. He thought the ship was killing him. Bleeding money. That is why he had named it *Prometheus* when the market crashed soon after he had bought it. The pain had never stopped since.

"Captain," he said smoothly. "Of course you are right. You are right to call me and not the operations manager. In our family we value loyal captains like you, from our home island. And of course you are right to consider security for the ship and your crew."

The traffic was edging forward now. He moved his head to one side to get a good look at the girl in the wing mirror. "Yes, Captain," he said. "I know Somalia is dangerous. I appreciate that a charter to take fuel to Kismayo is not ideal. But in this market it pays well and we must do it."

He was looking forward now. The girl had not smiled at him. Perhaps she had not recognised him after all. He thought he would call his public relations people and get some more photos of him out in the press. He did not want to drop out of the public eye. Not when he was about to launch his CanDo car hire firm. That would be the business that would make him rich. His CanDo leisure centres and his CanDo coffee shops hadn't quite performed as he wished. The market was always wrong. His shipping company, CanDoTank, was hurting him. But CanDoCars would work.

John C described himself on his business cards as a serial entrepreneur. He thought that the captain on his one ship did not respect his business empire. He was so wrapped up in his narrow little world of shipping. "Captain," he spoke a little more sharply now. "You must of course follow the recommended security measures. You must follow the internationally agreed Best Management Practices."

He paused. "Of course, Captain," he continued quietly. "You should interpret those Best Management Practices in light of the economic climate and bearing in mind that in this case the charterer's client has guaranteed us full security."

It was smooth and quiet and cool in the Range Rover. He could hear the captain's reply clearly. He thought that he had understood. He was not to spend any money on useless security measures.

The traffic was moving now and he would soon be at his private office. The office was in fact an apartment over his first leisure club, handily placed close to Mayfair. The rent was a little high, but he had to be in the right place. "Of course, Captain, I will give your best wishes to my father," he said. "Goodbye and have a good trip." He touched the phone switch on the wheel and wriggled in anticipation. Natasha would be waiting for him at the club. She had been the best personal trainer in his club. Now she was something even more personal in his apartment. The captain would be fine, and for once the ship would pay for itself this voyage. He forgot about the ship and thought about Natasha. That girl who had ignored him would die for a body like hers.

* * *

Yusuf was holding Abdi's arm and pointing at the pile of boxes and boats stacked under covers at the back of the beach. It was the cargo from the dhow.

"That boy on guard is Mo," said Yusuf. "And those boys there are from your clan too. Mo will tell you their names. We have to get to work. We have to get the boats ready. In one or two days we are going to sea. The weather will be good and we will take a ship. You will learn what it is to live in Somalia. *Inshallah*, you will learn how we make the foreign devils pay for their ships."

He could sense Abdi hanging back. He knew the boy did not want to go. The boy was a foreign devil himself. What did he know of Somalia? Nothing. He could hardly speak Somali. He looked at Abdi. He was taller and stronger than the local boys. Yusuf thought he would not be as tough.

He pushed Abdi hard. "We will fit the motors to the boats and begin to load them," he commanded. "You have a day to learn how to handle the boat. These boys can help you. You are going to marry my eldest daughter. These boys know that. I am a big man here. You must make them respect you. You will be in charge of one boat. Come, you will learn something you did not learn at school in Cardiff."

* * *

"Liverpool? Steven Gerrard?" said Abdi. "You follow Liverpool, Mo?"

Abdi had discovered the universal language. He was using his Somali but speaking Premier League. "What about Spurs, then? They are having a great season," he said.

He laughed at the replies. All the boys were speaking at once now. They are all Man U supporters, he thought. Knobs! "What about Cardiff City then, will we go up this year?" Blank faces told him that the Bluebirds weren't on the map for Somali boys. Stick to the Premier League, he thought. Not that this lot look top flight.

"Azi," he asked. "Have you got a ball? Let's have a kick about."

Abdi turned out every weekend for Cardiff Bay Warriors. With his height and build he was a handy centre back. He had noticed that the other teams were reluctant to tackle him. Off the pitch he was quiet, uncommitted. On the ball he was hard and quick. He liked winning.

On the beach now he quickly gained the respect of the boys. Azi was the tallest, but his slight frame bounced off Abdi when he tried a tackle. Mo was quick, but not as quick as Abdi. They can carry guns around but they can't hang onto the ball, thought Abdi.

When they saw Yusuf approaching the boys picked up the ball and went back to work. They were rigging the boats and motors. "Abdi," said Mo. He was pleased that they called his name now. "Come, we take this boat. We show you. Through the surf, back to the beach. Come on."

* * *

Yusuf crouched in the flat-bottomed skiff. It was on the beach, but had been moved close to the water's edge. He checked the batteries. He checked the electronic equipment. He turned over the shining new outboard motors. He was grinning to himself. Somalia is a broken country. But a man with money can get anything.

He turned to check the fuel drums. His back hurt as he bent. He thought he was getting too old for this. This would be his last trip, he promised himself. He would make enough money this time. Enough to pay off that Chinese bloodsucker in Dubai. Enough to pay off the parents of the boys lost when he had sent out boats too early into the bad monsoon. Enough to pay off the elders and politicians. Enough to finance more trips with younger men in the boat. He would control them from ashore. That was right for a man who had earned honour.

Yusuf sensed Abdi watching him. "Check everything with care, my son," he said. "These boys are careless. They drink and they chew quat before we go to sea. It makes them brave. Brave is good. But the leader must be brave and careful." Yes, he thought, and the leader will earn enough to pay for a big wedding for his eldest daughter.

Yusuf knew that a wedding for a man of his status would cost at least one hundred thousand dollars. He knew that he would have to pay twice the cost of everything he needed now for the ship hijack trip once he had money to pay. He knew that he would have to pay the boys who were guarding the boats and stores. He would have to pay the boys who came with him to find and hijack a ship. He would have to pay the boys who would guard the ship when it came in. The food for the hostages. The translators and negotiators. He needed half a million dollars from a hijack just to break even.

"Abdi," he spoke more loudly now, as Abdi was checking his boat over a few feet away. "You will see, this is not about money. It is protection of our coast. It is to stop foreigners making fools of Somalis. We cannot fish ourselves. We cannot trade. The country has no government, no money, no roads and nothing is safe. By charging the ships and fishing boats who come into our waters we bring cash to our boys. Cash to our villages. Money to build houses and ristorantes. Money to attract good men for our daughters. These shipowners can pay. They don't care, because they don't pay. They have insurance that can pay. No-one gets hurt. They respect Somalia."

And I will be able to pay for your wedding, to feel proud in front of Ahmed and the family again, he thought.

Yusuf looked up. Abdi was head down, busy. "Yes, Father," was all he heard.

.

CHAPTER FIVE

There were ten of them. Four with Yusuf in one boat, four with Abdi in the second boat. It was heavy work sliding the loaded boats down the sand and through the surf. The boys were slow and not pulling their weight. They came through the surf and climbed on board, shivering in the cool of the morning. There was hardly room to squat between the drums of water and fuel. Abdi thought that there was not much food. Tins of tuna and bags of pasta and a sack of rice. He saw they had bags of quat. They chew that to keep off the hunger, he thought. I don't want to do that. I hope we won't be out here too long. What happens if I get seasick? What happens if I need a dump? How the hell do they do that out there on this tiny boat?

Mo and Azi both had hangovers. Abdi looked at the other boys. They all had red eyes. I thought I was coming to a Muslim country, Abdi said to himself. At home some of his friends drank. Most of them didn't, and a lot of the boys at school had grown beards now and become strict against alcohol and drugs. They talked about *jihad* and their global Muslim brotherhood. Abdi listened to them but didn't talk. He didn't drink because he was saving his money for university, not for global Islamic domination. They would have a shock if they saw these Muslims, thought Abdi.

He looked up. Yusuf was shouting and waving him forward. His boat accelerated and headed out to sea. Abdi turned the twist grip and swung to follow him. He shivered. Maybe I should have spent more time in the mosque, he thought.

* * *

Lisa was leaning on the bridge wing rail. Two miles away the heat haze shimmered over the coast of Oman. Beneath her feet the ship was quiet. They were drifting. The captain had stopped the ship there an hour ago, then made two long calls in Greek to the office. "Our security is coming," he told her enigmatically as he left the bridge. "Call me when you see a dhow approaching."

Lisa was bored and fed up. On Norwegian ships women were commonplace. On Norwegian ships she had young companions to pass her off watch time with. On the *Prometheus* she was a novelty. A confident, direct young woman. The crew did not know how to deal with her. And she did not want to give any of them ideas.

She did not know what the captain meant by security. He had told her they were carrying oil for Somalia, but she could see no sign of any security measures. He had reassured her, security would be there. And he had reminded her that there was extra pay for the two voyages they were chartered for.

In the distance she saw the black speck of a dhow crawling over the sea towards them. Behind it the dry red cliffs were nothing like the soft green hills of her home on the west coast of Norway. In Ulsteinvik she had looked out at the rain and dreamt of following her father as a captain at sea. She had dreamt of working on the ships she saw built at the

Kleven and Ulstein yards across from her house. Not much of a dream now, Lisa, she told herself as she reached for the intercom to the captain's cabin. You are on a dirty little ship on a dirty little trade.

"The dhow is coming, Captain," she said.

Puttering alongside, the dhow was almost at the same level as the deck of the *Prometheus*. Four skinny youths in tee shirts and tracksuit bottoms swung themselves up and over the rail onto the foredeck. They carried a bundle in one hand and a Kalashnikov in the other. Lisa thought they looked exactly like all the photos of Somali pirates.

"Our security," said the captain drily. "Not that we need them. Our security is that every bandit in Somalia knows that we are carrying oil for Al Shabab. No-one will attack us. That is our security."

The dhow moved clear and Lisa pushed the ship's engine control ahead, setting course for Kismayo. She wasn't happy. An oil cargo for an Islamist guerrilla movement in southern Somalia. Four pirates with guns to protect them. But she could not get off now. And if the men could do it, so could she.

* * *

Yusuf whispered it to himself. "*Inshallah*. This is the one." He had been bent over the portable AIS transceiver, fiddling with the battery connections while one of the boys held a torch. The screen settled down and there was the display he wanted to see. The Automatic Identification System is a great tool for pirates. The United Nations obliges 40,000 ships globally to use AIS every time they move. It broadcasts their position and a lot of other information every few seconds. It is intended to help reduce collisions at sea and it is encouraged by coastal states as an anti-terrorist

25

security system. It also tells any pirate with a set that can be bought for a few hundred dollars the exact position of any ship within 50 miles. Better still, it tells the hijacker what the ship is carrying and where it is going, and how to intercept it.

The skiffs had spent the night stopped, bobbing gently a few yards apart in the slight seas. Now in the pre-dawn Yusuf had found his target. The screen showed her 25 miles to the North and headed South South West. The Maltese flag tanker *Elouise* was loaded with 106,000 tonnes of heavy fuel oil and headed for Dar es Salaam. The AIS display updated every six minutes. The ship was big, 243 metres long, it was loaded with valuable oil, and it was coming towards the skiffs at a steady 14 knots.

Yusuf called Abdi to come alongside. The two boats ground together as he struggled to steer, half asleep, muzzy-headed with seasickness and afraid of what was going to happen next. Two boys held the boats together while Yusuf spoke quietly and clearly to everyone. "Our money is coming now," he grinned. "Big money. From this way. The ship is big, but loaded. We go together, then one boat each side at the stern. Keep quiet and we can get aboard while they sleep. The first one of you on the deck with his gun will be driving a new Toyota when we reach the land. And all of you will be with the girl you dream of that night. Go with God."

Waving to Abdi to follow, Yusuf fired up his outboard and began to run the interception course obligingly displayed on the AIS.

.

CHAPTER SIX

Andrei Grimov was unhappy. He was steadily pulling chin-ups on the bar he had set into his cabin doorway. His thin and heavily-tattooed arms lifted his scrawny frame with ease. Doing chin-ups bored him, but like so many Russian veterans of his age, it was what he did. On the ship all he did was clean and test his weapons, pull chin-ups and watch YouTube videos of Russian naval commandos killing Somali pirates. There was no internet connection now at sea, it was too early to make noise with the guns, so he pulled chin-ups.

He thought that the *Elouise* had cleared the pirate zone without a chance to fire in earnest. Since boarding the ship from the anonymous dhow used by Russian security guards off Djibouti he had fired his AK-74 rifle twice. He had fired his PKM light machine gun twice. But the only targets were rubbish bags dumped over the side by the cook. Andrei wanted a real target. He wanted to kill some Arabs.

Now the ship was out of the Gulf of Aden and would soon be close to Tanzania and he would again be off the ship, waiting bored for a north-bound Russian-owned vessel to guard on its voyage past the Somali coast.

The alarm came just as he was dropping for the 100th time. He finished the lift, counted 101 and ran for the bridge, just behind the two other skin-headed guards who were coming out of their cabins and heading the same way.

The three men pulled their weapons from the locked cabinet behind the bridge. Andrei slowed slightly to let the others grab the AK-74 rifles. He wanted the PKM. The PKM is a 7.62 mm general-purpose machine gun designed in the Soviet Union and it was the standard light machine gun in use when Andrei had fought in the Second Chechen war. Andrei knew the AK-74 could kill at 600 metres. And he knew that the PKM could kill with much greater accuracy at 1,600 metres. He wanted to kill.

The grey-haired Ukrainian captain did not like Andrei and his fellow guards, but he was always careful to hide his feelings. He was glad of them now. He pointed away from the port quarter, half behind and to one side of the ship's spreading wake. Andrei was not offered the captain's binoculars, but he didn't need them. Out of the grey light lifting over the sea two white skiffs were accelerating towards the ship. He could see dark figures in them, and the outline of an RPG. He bent over the PKM, finding the skiffs in the sight.

In the bridge house the officer of the watch was on the radio to the Russian frigate which had stayed with them through the Gulf of Aden. It was too far away to help now but would alert any naval units in the area. There were 43 warships organised into three naval task forces in the area. Most seafarers thought they were doing nothing, and most pirates shared their view. But the Russian, Indian and Chinese navies looked after their own.

The crew of the *Elouise* expected help from the Russian Navy because the ship was owned and run by

Severflot, a Russian state-owned firm with close ties to the Swiss bank accounts of the Kremlin power elite. The ship had an English girl's name, flew the Maltese flag, was managed out of Cyprus and the crew were all Ukrainian. That is standard in a shipping world where tax matters more than nationality. But the ship was a Russian enterprise.

Russia looks after its ships. The *Elouise* was protected on this voyage, and on every voyage, by the Russian Navy frigates, by private armed guards on board and by the fierce reputation of the Russians for hitting back hard at pirates who captured their ships. Had Yusuf's AIS told him it was a Russian ship he would not have attacked.

The captain spoke to Andrei first. "You fire when I tell you," he said. "Not before." There was one guard with them on this side of the ship, his AK-74 held and sighted. The other was ready on the starboard bridge wing. The captain tapped the guard's Kalashnikov. "Put some bullets close to them," he said.

The AK-74 can fire 700 rounds per minute but has only a 30-round standard magazine. The standard Russian infantry weapon, it is tough and simple. But fired from a standing position on a moving ship at a high-speed skiff the chance of actually hitting anything is remote. The gun barked in short bursts of three, and from the bridge Andrei could see spurts of water lifting near the boats. He saw the boats swerve closer together and cursed as he thought one seemed to slow.

But then they came on, pushing towards the ship's wake, and Andrei grinned as he swung the PKM to follow them.

* * *

Abdi was shaking. The flat bottom of the skiff was

slapping over the waves, pushed by the screaming outboard at full throttle. Azi was balanced on one side of the skiff, shouting and pointing at the ship. Mo and the other boys were bracing themselves as they pulled boarding ladders and grapnel lines out ready to throw onto the ship's deck. Abdi felt the boat shaking, felt the engine vibrating, felt his stomach falling as the ship came quickly closer.

Ahead of them Abdi saw water spiking in a line. Then again to the right. And again. "Faster!" screamed Azi. He was standing up now. "They have guns. Go faster!"

Abdi swerved the boat towards Yusuf and began to slow. Surely they wouldn't attack an alert ship which was shooting at them? He heard Azi screaming, "Faster!" The air cracked as Azi fired a wild burst from his Kalashnikov. And in the other skiff he saw Yusuf urging him on with a clenched fist, while his boys stood up ready to grapple to the ship.

Abdi gunned the throttle open and swung the skiff towards the ship's wake again. The attack was going in and he was going to be a pirate.

* * *

On the bridge of the *Elouise* the captain ordered the officer of the watch to fishtail. Swinging the ship right and left at full speed makes it hard for skiffs to get close enough to board.

Andrei felt the ship swing to starboard and saw the skiffs disappearing behind the funnel. He was pulling the PKM from its mountings to run through the bridge when he felt the captain's restraining hand. "Wait," he said.

Then as the ship swung back to port both skiffs came into view, close now and closing fast. The captain spoke slowly and quietly to Andrei. "OK, OMONchnik," he said. "It's your turn. Give them the full Medvedev."

Andrei grinned. President Medvedev had gone up lot in his estimation since he had been quoted in the news saying that as no international law existed to prosecute pirates, "they would have to act as their forefathers did when they met pirates."

Andrei had done two things to his PKM. He had mounted a telescopic sight and spent time making sure it was lined up. And he had taped a video camera to the stock. He wanted his own YouTube video.

Now he reached forward, checked the video was running, and brought the gun up to his shoulder. In the sight he caught the bow of the closest boat. He checked his breath and slowly, happily, squeezed the trigger.

The captain called Andrei OMONchnik because of his background fighting in Chechnya as a conscript with the low-life Interior Ministry paramilitaries, OMON. That time had taught Andrei two things. One was to hate all Arabs, which meant anyone black. The second was that you killed more of them when you were careful and methodical. So Andrei applied his lessons well, squeezing and relaxing the trigger gently to put short bursts into the boat.

He saw the wood flying up as the bullets cut into the bow, then one figure thrown backwards into the sea by the impact. Tracking down he fired again, watching the drums he could see in the boat moving and then two dark figures doubling over.

"That's three on account," he said to himself. He was reliving the ambush that had left thirty of his OMON comrades, all conscripts from his home city of Perm, dead on a Chechen hillside. He eased the gun upwards slightly to further even the score, but the ship was swinging back to starboard and he swore as the funnel again blocked his view.

* * *

Abdi shut the engine throttle down as he felt the bullets hitting the boat. He saw Azi tumble backwards into the sea. Then the boat shook again and Mo doubled over. Abdi felt wetness on his leg as the drums just ahead of him took the bullets. Then the boat stopped and the sudden silence was broken by a long shuddering moan from underneath Mo.

Yusuf was slowing and turning towards them. Abdi saw the ship swing back as it straightened its course. He could clearly read the ship's name and home port, Valetta, on the stern. He braced himself, trying to control his bladder. But the ship was moving away fast now and there were no more bullets.

The boat was filling with water quickly. Abdi lunged forward, lifting Mo into a sitting position. Under him was one of the new boys. Or what was left of him. Four rounds of PKM ammunition had taken off the side of his head and smashed his chest open.

In the water Abdi could see a frenzy of sharks worrying at Azi's body. But he had no time to imagine what would happen next. Yusuf's skiff banged alongside and desperate hands grabbed the boats together. "Come quick, son," yelled Yusuf. "Get in here, get what you can in here."

Mo was lifted into Yusuf's boat. Abdi saw that he did not scream as his shattered leg caught the bulwarks. He reached down for the dead boy but was checked by Yusuf. "We go, be quick, he is dead," he said. So Abdi clambered over the body and was half pulled and half fell into the bottom of Yusuf's boat. His boys were grabbing for barrels of fuel and water from Abdi's skiff, but it sank too quickly.

CHAPTER SEVEN

The only sound was the waves rippling against the boat. Yusuf had killed the engine and made a quick inspection of the boat. There were now eight of them crowded between the drums of oil and water. Mo was lying stretched out on the only open space. His breath came in sharp rasps. Abdi saw that someone had tied off his leg and staunched the bleeding.

Abdi was tense, expecting shouting and recrimination, an argument, anything. But the boys arranged themselves silently and listened as Yusuf spoke. "We have food and water for two days, and fuel for one more attack," he said quietly. "We can find another ship, and with God's will we will capture it."

The boys looked at Abdi as he burst out. "For God's sake, what about Mo? This is crazy. We need food, we need water, we need fuel. The boat will be slow with the extra people in it. Azi is dead. We should go back."

He looked around the faces. They were all red eyed, from the sea wind and from the quat they had been chewing since leaving the beach. They looked at him, and thought him weak. He was big, but he did not know how to survive. He was big, but he was afraid. He was to be Yusuf's son, but he wanted to go back. He was to be Yusuf's son, but he had spoken without respect.

Yusuf waited for someone else to speak. When they did not, he spoke again, "*Ma fis*. It doesn't matter. I know where we will find a ship. And tomorrow, Abdi, you will be first on the deck." His voice was flat, emotionless. Gesturing for the GPS he fired up the engine and set the boat moving slowly South and West. Abdi thought Yusuf knew where he was heading, and he thought he was going there reluctantly. But he could not ask.

Yusuf knew the truth. They had to strike and capture a ship. If not, they were going to die. There had not been enough money to buy the fuel they needed and he had taken the boats out to hunt far beyond return range. Now they had lost one boat and were heavier than before. The coast was out of range. He had sent other boys out to die like this. To fight over the last drops of water as they drifted. Now it was his turn.

The quat supplies were holding out. And the quat was doing to Yusuf's mind what it always did. Clearing out any sense of fear or logic. He felt himself on fire. He felt young again. And he knew where he would find a valuable ship.

Stabbing at the GPS Yusuf calculated the course and speed he needed. It would take them to a point on the track ships coming down the Somali coast to Kismayo port would use. He had all that day and all the night to get there. The run would use most of their fuel, even at an economical speed. But there would be enough for one attack at high speed.

He knew that attack would be dangerous. But it was his only chance to win a ship and cargo. To win money. To pay Ah Hing. To give Amina the marriage she wanted. To make the elders and politicians treat him with respect. And there was no other way. This was a bad ship, but it was the only ship he could attack.

Yusuf set the course and with the engine on slow revs the boat was quiet. He looked up and laughed. He pointed his Kalashnikov into the sky, held up with one hand. The sudden burst of gunfire made Abdi jump. "Eat," Yusuf shouted. "Drink tea. Tomorrow morning we are rich."

* * *

Mo had been silent most of the day and through the night. The boat had pushed slowly South West, Yusuf always alert to his GPS, stopping three times to refuel the outboard tanks from the drums. Abdi had given Mo sips of sweet tea and quat to chew. But now as the boat lay stopped, wallowing in the slight seas, Abdi heard him moaning softly. Cold dew was wetting the bottom of the boat where Mo was lying. It wetted Abdi's thin shirt and he shivered in the light wind.

Yusuf was alert, listening. He pushed Mo with his foot. "Be quiet." Then Abdi heard it. A steady low thump carrying across the water. Yusuf tapped his gun butt on the gunwale, startling the half-asleep pirates into life. "Awake. Quiet now, then we go. Abdi first," he said.

Away to the east of the boat Abdi could see the dark outline of a ship against the dawn. It showed no lights. Abdi saw that Yusuf had not switched on the AIS. His mind was full of questions. What was the ship? How did Yusuf know it would be here? Could he jump on board? What would he do if the crew fought back? Why was Yusuf waiting now?

The pirates sat low in the silent boat, weapons tucked down, invisible in the darkness to anyone watching from the ship. Abdi was cramped and muzzy-headed, seasick and dehydrated. His stomach felt tight. The ship passed them slowly. It seemed a long time before Yusuf reached down and started the engine. Then the boat swung quickly, coming up to full speed right behind the ship. It hurtled forward, bobbing in the confused wake. Abdi checked his Kalashnikov and in a reflex action, reached down to tighten his laces. He almost laughed, this wasn't football in Bute Park.

CHAPTER EIGHT

Fully loaded, the *Prometheus* was designed to make 13 knots. But age and poor maintenance had cut that to 11 knots on a good day with the wind behind her. Fully loaded she had a design freeboard of 1.45 metres. So the deck edge was only five feet from the waterline. If she had been observing the Best Management Practices she would have barbed wire strung along the side rails. But the captain had understood John Canopoulos well. Barbed wire costs money, so there was no barbed wire.

Slow, low in the water and not hardened to attack, the *Prometheus* was the ideal pirate target. Except that pirates did not attack it. Like Yusuf, they knew the ship was carrying fuel for Al Shabab. They knew it would be well guarded. Their mobile phones had crackled for months with warnings of the consequences of interfering with Al Shabab supply lines. They could find foreign ships whose owners would pay up quietly and quickly. They did not want to face an assault by Al Shabab trying to get their cargo back. So the *Prometheus* slipped quietly about its business, unmolested.

In Somali waters nothing is so clear cut. The strong overcome the weak. It was the start of Ramadan, and Yusuf thought that Ramadan was a good time to attack Islamists. And any ship was good if you had enough guns to defend it until the owner paid the ransom. There is no honour amongst thieves.

There was no sign of movement on the ship as Yusuf thrust the bow right into the curling wake alongside the lowest part of the deck. As the boat slammed against the ship Abdi saw the hooked boarding ladder thrown up onto the deck edge. He felt Yusuf's Kalashnikov push hard into his back. Then he was up, jumping onto a drum, onto the ladder and in two steps he was over the rail onto the ship's deck.

Behind him Abdi could hear the others tumbling onto the deck. Ahead were the steps leading up to the accommodation block. Pushing his Kalashnikov in front Abdi ran aft. He was going to be first on the bridge. He would not be looked at again as a coward.

Abdi had swung round from one ladder to climb the next. He could see the bridge three decks above. Two strides took him up six steel steps. There was a bright flash and heavy crack right ahead of him. At the top of the steeply-angled ladder a dark figure was spraying gunfire down on him.

He wasn't stopping now. His finger squeezed the trigger, the gun jumped and Abdi was up and over the body, looking for the next stairway. Breathing hard, he felt the adrenalin pumping through him. There was more shooting above him. Abdi checked himself for a second as bullets whined off the steel bulkheads beside him. Then he was firing again, short bursts as Yusuf had shown him. Aimed bursts. And then leaping up the steps, tripping over another body and pulling himself upright to charge into the bridge.

Three men were there. Hands held high, shouting. Abdi heard it in English and Somali. "Don't shoot." He held his gun on them, poised, heart thumping. He did not know what to do next.

* * *

Lisa always slept with the door locked. She had been working on all-male ships for four years. She wasn't afraid of the men she sailed with. But they were men and away from home. She knew she always had to be dressed or behind a locked door.

When the gunfire woke her she grabbed for the overalls she put handy every night. Whatever was happening she would face it clothed. Her mouth was dry as she buttoned up the orange boiler suit and slipped on her work boots. Her instinct was to run for the bridge. On Norwegian ships there was a pirate drill and a safe citadel to hide in. But here there was no citadel and no drill. Just the scrawny Somali youths in their mixed-up clothes and guns too big for them as guards.

The shooting had stopped. Lisa hesitated. Was she safer here or should she go to help? Then the door shook as the handle was shaken hard from outside. "Out, out," she heard. It was not a crewman. Lisa slipped back the lock and the door burst open. She was looking down the barrel of a gun, and the man holding it was red-eyed and frantic.

* * *

Yusuf was a new man. He was barking orders, pushing the boys, laughing out loud. Abdi watched as two of the three men in the bridge were forced to the deck and tied up. Yusuf had his gun hard in the back of the taller man. He was not Somali, Abdi thought. A ship's officer. Yusuf was yelling at him. "Set course to North. Ship goes to Harardhere. Fast, quick."

On the deck below the bridge Abdi could see two more of Yusuf's boys herding the crew out of the accommodation. The skiff was still tied alongside, bumping in the wake. Mo was lying there, shaking each time the boat surged against the steel side of the ship. And behind him on the ship Abdi could see the two bodies. Both wore orange overalls with 'Prometheus' across the back. He thought he had shot the crew. His hands shook.

Yusuf was shouting his name now. "Abdi! Son! No dreaming! Those boys no good. Al Shabab. Throw them into the sea. Then we get Mo and we go home. You marry Amina soon."

It is hard to lift a dead body. Harder still when it is the first person you have ever killed. Abdi was doing what he was told, and he dragged the bodies to the rail and tumbled them over into the sea. He saw he had killed two teenagers. Not older than him. Somali boys who had taken or been given a set of crew overalls. He looked at himself. What would they have seen if they had killed him? Would they have seen an armed sea robber? Or a young Welshman who wanted to go to university? Who wanted a career in a warm, clean optician's practice?

.

CHAPTER NINE

Lisa was standing beside the captain. Looking around she could see seven other crew, huddled together on the foredeck, most dressed like her, in company overalls grabbed in a hurry. She knew the second engineer was in the engine room and the chief mate was on the bridge. She had handed over the watch to him at 0400. "A quiet night," she had told him, "nothing on the radar, nothing about," before going down to sleep.

They were all safe, but afraid. The pirates were jumpy, watching them closely. They were careless with their weapons, swinging round, shouting at each other, excited. Lisa thought they were like children. Naughty children. She thought they were taking turns to ransack the cabins. Two at a time they disappeared, then came back wearing watches she recognised, the East German tracksuits the crew favoured. Then one was showing off, hand on hip, wearing her bra.

Lisa lunged forward. Her underwear was not up for grabs. The smack of the gun barrel across her neck took her by surprise, forcing her to the deck. "You. No move. You woman?" she heard. "Woman?" She could smell his sweat. Lisa shouted back. "Yes, woman. Don't touch my clothes. Get off me."

The pirate stepped back, allowing Lisa to scramble to her feet. Now they were all looking at her. She could not understand what they were saying. She did not want to imagine. "Don't touch my clothes," she repeated. She was angry.

* * *

Abdi was feeling better about himself. He had killed two boys, but he had to do it. They were terrorists and they would have killed him. And it felt good to have led the boarding, to have charged the bridge first. They would look at him in a different way now.

He stepped down from the bridge ladders. He was going to call for help to get Mo on board and comfortable. On the deck he sensed the tension, heard the clamour, but in the excitement he could not make sense of the dialect. He thought they were talking about a woman, but there were no women here.

Then he heard her voice, angry, clear, sounding Swedish. "I said don't touch my ploody clothes, you ape." And as he pushed through the boys he saw her. Short blond hair, dressed like the others. But as she thrust forward defiantly, very clearly a woman.

"You are a woman," said Abdi. "What do you do here?"

"I'm an officer, and these apes are stealing my clothes," he heard.

Abdi was confused. He did not know that women worked as ship's officers. He did not know that Somali pirates were also common thieves. Yusuf had told him it was about protecting the Somali coast. About foreign ships abusing Somalia's waters. About stopping Al Shabab.

The boys were silent, watching him. He would be Yusuf's son. He had killed today. They saw his eyes moving over them. He was looking at their purloined clothes. At the watches they had not been wearing when they boarded. They saw disgust on his face.

Abdi was not angry with the boys. He was angry with himself. He was not a coastguard hero. He was a common thief. An armed robber. It wasn't a good feeling.

His self-disgust lent strength to his voice. "*Haram,*" he said in his lilting Somali, turning to make sure all the boys heard him. "This woman is *haram.* You don't touch her. You don't touch her clothes. You don't touch anything of her. Forbidden." Abdi turned to Lisa. "Best not to shout, isn't it," he said. "Sit down and be quiet. You are safe now."

* * *

Yusuf saw Abdi facing down the boys. He saw him send them to lift Mo carefully aboard and make him comfortable in a cabin. He saw the wake of the ship widening as it came up to speed, heading for Harardhere. He saw the money and power the ship would bring. He saw Nadifa choosing a new *dirac* for the wedding. He saw himself walking amongst the wedding guests, distributing *sooryo,* fresh green dollar bills for everyone. He saw a son who was tougher than he had thought, and he was happy. Happy for himself, and happy for Amina. She needed a strong man to control and protect her.

And a woman in the crew. Yusuf thought this was useful. She would be a valuable hostage. More money, and the money would come quicker. Westerners were fools like that, they paid more for a woman than for a man. But she would also be trouble. His boys were not used to a woman amongst them.

He was glad he had Abdi. Abdi understood Western women. He would make the woman behave and keep her from tempting the boys. He would keep her safe, because safe she was worth money.

Yusuf had his gun pushed hard into the captain's back. "Go closer, Captain," he ordered. "Anchor close to shore." The captain was trying to explain something about draft and shoals, but Yusuf was getting angry. He wanted the ship anchored close to the beach. It was easier to protect then, easier to get to and from. He wanted it close, because it was his ship now and he did not want anyone to take it away from him.

Abdi was at the back of the bridge. He did not know anything about ships. But he knew the captain was not happy to go further. "Father, the captain says the ship is not safe if we go close to the beach," he translated. "He says we must stay this far from the shore. If not we touch the bottom, spill the oil, don't we."

Yusuf thought that the ship was small and could go closer. But his son had spoken to him with respect, and the others had heard. "OK, Captain," he growled. "Anchor now. Here."

As the captain gave the order to drop the anchor Yusuf turned to Abdi.

"You will keep the woman in one cabin," he ordered. "Our men must not see her. All crew sleep in captain's cabin, only her alone. You take her food. No-one else. We will not wait too long for our money, *Inshallah*."

Then suddenly happy, he turned to the captain. "Anchor OK, Captain? Now satphone. Come quick. We call office. My son Abdi will talk. Your company pay five million US dollars. Then you go home. No shit. No pay, you die."

CHAPTER TEN

John Canopoulos was raging. He had been enjoying some very personal training with Natasha when his phone had rung the first time. His damned wife only called him when she was bored, which seemed to be all the time. And she insisted on speaking Greek. Of course, he thought, she is Greek, and looks it. He had married her because his father and her father were close. She came with a lot of money. She had everything she could want in their villa in Vouliagmeni. John C could not quite form the thought, but he despised Greeks just a little. His education at Charterhouse and the business career his father had helped him with in London made him feel more British than Greek.

He had been polite to her. Polite even when she pointed out that he was losing money. Polite even when she brought up what her father advised, and what his father also advised. Polite even when she recalled that he had sold the ships his father gave him when the market was low and only bought back into shipping when the market was booming and values were at an all-time high. What was her point? Her point was that her father had advised her not to allow any more of her money to be used to back his ventures. Her point was she was shafting CanDoCars because he needed her money to launch it and he was not having any more of her money. But he was still polite, even when he said goodbye after promising to fly to Athens to talk it over with her.

He turned back to Natasha. She had a big smile as she reached out for him. At 42 he thought he still had a good body. Natasha seemed to like it, even if his wife didn't. Perhaps he was carrying a little more weight than he should, he thought. But he did not have any trouble attracting girls with great bodies like Natasha. And when he was in Greece there was no shortage of models to hang on his arm when he went out. Perhaps that was what was bothering his wife? He would go to Athens, take her to bed, sort her out.

Then the phone rang again. It was his operations manager. John C liked talking to him even less than he did talking to the captain. These calls were always expensive.

"Mr Canopoulos," he heard. The manager was clearly in a panic. "I have something serious to report. I have had a call from the *Prometheus*. She has been captured by Somali pirates. They are demanding a five million US dollar ransom."

John C did not want to believe it. First his fucking wife shafting his great new car hire business, and now the fucking darkies shafting his ship's first profitable charter in two years.

"There is no doubt, I am sorry, Mr Canopoulos," the manager was saying deferentially. "I have checked the ship AIS tracking and it is switched off. I spoke with the captain and also with one of the pirates. He spoke very good English. They have the ship, they have the cargo and they won't be letting it go until they get five million US dollars."

"Get hold of the navy, they are supposed to be looking after our shipping," shouted John C. "Find out what happened. Why can't they get in and take out these pirates? And get hold of the insurance broker, I want to know what the insurance covers."

He cut the phone but it rang as soon as he lifted his finger from the button. He saw that it was his cousin. His cousin was chief executive of Vexol, a major oil trading company. He breathed in and calmed his voice. He needed the business his cousin gave him.

"Hi, Yannis," he said breezily. "How can I help?"

He thought he had sounded helpful and confident. Clearly his cousin was not in the mood for helpful and confident today. Had he not been told? What was he doing about it? Vexol had sold a cargo of 6,000 tonnes of fuel to Al Shabab. He had trusted John C and his miserable ship to deliver it. He had paid him three times the market rate to deliver it. But he hadn't delivered it. Al Shabab was angry, they knew the cargo had been hijacked. How could he help? He could help by getting his bloody ship moving again, and quickly.

John C thought life was unfair. Natasha would have to wait. Right now he supposed he had better show up at the shipping company office. He would think of a way out of this. How did that stupid captain let his ship get captured anyway?

* * *

Yusuf looked at the half circle of men and boys. He would have wanted more. The loss of Azi and the others was bad. Taking an Al Shabab ship was bad. There was talk in all the villages. The usual rush to volunteer to guard a hijacked ship had not come.

"We have good weapons, we have plenty of ammunition," he said. He wanted to give them confidence.

"We will not stay in the village. We will build a camp here, in the cliffs. From there we can watch our boats and from there we can see our ship. There is only one way to the beach, and we can stop anyone with an RPG."

The response was muted. The boys looked uncertain. There were no questions. Somalis respect their elders but they love to discuss plans and orders. When a Somali does not question a decision by the leader then things are going badly wrong. Yusuf spoke again. "We are few, but we are strong," he said. "There will be more money each. The cowards will sit at home. The cowards will marry the ugly girls. You will be rich. In your villages they will respect you. The virgins will come to your bed."

He saw some grins now. Quickly he set out the routines. The camp there. The stores there. The skiffs to supply the ship there and there, not too close together. One guard at the top of the cliff. One guard with an RPG where the road narrowed to dip down to the beach. The other RPG here, to protect the boats. You and you and you will use the jeeps, keep the camp and ship supplied. You and you and you will go for the quat, meet the planes which we will fly in from Kenya with fresh quat. That made the grins widen.

"Abdi, you will make sure the ship is kept safe. You can speak with those people. If they behave they will live. That ship is the future for you and Amina. You look after it," he said.

Abdi was standing to one side. He felt flat. He was a pirate now. It was bullshit about protecting the seas. Yusuf was a thief. He was a thief who was afraid of other thieves stealing what he had stolen. Abdi thought that Yusuf was not just a thief, he was not even a good thief. He could see that the other boys did not trust him.

The weight of the Kalashnikov almost felt natural

now. Was this his future? A thief with a gun. A thief who would not sleep at home because other thieves would rob him. Abdi looked around at the beach. It felt a long way from Cardiff. He thought he would not be able to tell anyone at Cardiff University about this. He could not tell his father or his mother. If he tried to tell his football team they would think he was a bullshitter. He could not tell his friends who listened to the Islamic preachers on the internet. They would call him a traitor, a blasphemer.

Abdi shook himself. He was here now. He had to stay alive. He had to make this ransom work. Then he could marry Amina and go back to Cardiff. He had a different future there.

CHAPTER ELEVEN

Yusuf's house looked welcoming now. Abdi had thought it was a wreck when he had first seen it. After the days at sea and the attacks, it looked like paradise. The servant girl brought him warm water and he washed carefully. As he dressed he could hear giggling. It sounded like Amina. He felt himself getting an erection.

He pulled on a clean white shirt and khaki trousers and waited, embarrassed, for the swelling in his pants to go down. As he stepped through into the large front room he saw Amina. She was standing. The light from the door was behind her. He caught his breath. The girls at home wear tight jeans, he thought. My sisters wear their headscarves like jewellery. They were always talking about boys.

If they want the boys to look at them they should try these long gowns, he thought. Amina was walking towards him now. Slowly, head slightly down. He was fixed to the spot. He could see she was looking at him through her eyelashes. Her eyes were sparkling. "You were the first on board," she said. "My father told me. You are strong, very strong."

She was close to him now. Looking up at him. Not touching, but close enough that he could have touched her if he had reached out. He could not move his hand. He was afraid he would get an erection again. He had a lump in his throat. He could not speak. Amina turned away to sit down. "Sit," she said. "You will be my husband. I will be proud of you." Abdi thought she was laughing at him.

Amina's mother was in the room now. Yusuf was behind her, shouting for servants. There was much to celebrate. Tonight was to celebrate. Tomorrow Abdi must go back to guard the ship. Tonight he had a son and his daughter could plan her marriage. It was a good night.

* * *

The two goats were struggling as they were lifted from the skiff up and over the ship's rail. One of them sprayed the boat and boys below him with shit. Abdi laughed with the other boys on deck. That was their meat ration for a few days. It was Ramadan so they would eat one big meal each day, when the sun set. The goats would live on the deck, tied to the rail and kept quiet with a bundle of straw until they were butchered for goat and rice. Or goat and pasta, thought Abdi. No chance of a kebab or some fried chicken. He wished he was back in Cardiff.

He felt tired this morning. Last night they had sat for hours while members of the clan called. Everyone wanted to eat and drink and meet the boy who would be Yusuf's son. The boy who had been first on board the ship. He was treated with respect. Treated as a hero. And Amina had been there. When the visitors came she was careful to cover her hair and face. But Abdi knew her eyes were following him.

Yusuf had roused him early. They had bumped down the track to the beach, checked the guards at the beach camp and smashed out through the heavy surf to bring food to the ship. Abdi was sitting on the mooring bitt, planning the guard rota. The boys were all squatting on the steel deck around him, guns held vertical.

There should be six of them, he thought. That is the plan. They need to work in shifts, one on deck and one watching the crew all the time. He could see only five boys. "Where is the other boy," he asked, sharply. There was no reply. Only a low snigger.

Abdi was up and pushing his way towards the accommodation. He could see the boy now, peering through a window. He had his face up to the window and as he came closer Abdi could see he was trying to look through a gap in the curtains. One hand held his rifle. The other was down the front of his tracksuit trousers.

He didn't hesitate. He lifted his Kalashnikov and fired. The bullets whipped past the boy, who fell backwards, his hand still inside his trousers. "I told you, she is *haram*," Abdi said, pushing the boy with his foot. "You want a woman you can go away now. Go home. Or get one of the other boys to play with you. Leave this woman alone. She is money for us all."

The boy scrambled to his feet and shambled off to join the others. Abdi could see he had made an enemy, but he did not care. He heard a sound behind him and turned quickly.

She was there. Standing up straight. Looking directly at him. He could see her breasts pushing at the orange overall. She did not look afraid, he thought.

"You must cover your hair when you come outside," he said. "And you must make sure this curtain is properly closed. They are not used to having a girl with them." Neither am I, thought Abdi. She must be a very strong woman to work on the ship. He thought he would like to know more about her.

"We will talk later," he said. "Stay in your cabin now. When the guards are set and the ship is calm we will talk."

* * *

Lisa stared at the toilet bowl. She could not be sick again. Then she retched and felt the nausea right through her stomach. It was not just nausea. It was cold, hard fear that she felt.

Her last night in Oslo before she flew out to join the ship. Ole was such a sweet boy. He had a good job as a shipbroker. Clean, clear features, strong shoulders and unlike the boys she knew in Ulsteinvik, he danced. He danced well, and the beers they had enjoyed in the evening sunshine in the bar on the Aker Brygge, then the aquavit in the club had loosened them both up. Too loose, because they had been careless later, back in her hotel room.

Now I'm pregnant, she thought. Stuck on this foul little ship with these bloody thugs, and I'm pregnant. She was close to tears.

Lisa retched again then stood up and carefully took some water from the bucket to clean her mouth. She looked in the mirror. Every officer's cabin had a small bathroom and she could still use hers, although the taps and shower no longer ran. You are strong, she told herself. You may not be the best looker, but boys like you. You do a real job at sea. You are an officer. Maybe Ole will be happy about the baby. Ships are always ransomed quickly. CanDoTank is a good company. Canopoulos is a good owner. He will look after the captain, and we will be on our way soon. Then I can leave the ship and go back to Norway. No-one need know.

She straightened her back and made sure her overall

was buttoned up fully. Using the mirror she made sure none of her short blond hair showed beneath the scarf she had tied it up in. She was going on watch. It was just another day. No-one will know, she told herself. But she knew. She felt fear and hope, and did not know which was strongest.

.

CHAPTER TWELVE

John C was alone in his office. Outside he could hear the operations manager on the phone. He was aware that the sexy little receptionist he had promised the job to was at her desk. He had noticed her tight hot pants when he came in. He tried not to think about her now. He was looking at the insurance documents of the ship. He began to smile.

He thought the captain had been careless to let himself get hijacked. He thought that it would hurt him with Vexol. His cousin was not happy. But his cousin would have the cargo insured. And insurance was making John C's day.

He went through the documents again. The *Prometheus* was insured with the Norway-based Scandinavian Club. They had been happy to get his business. He thought that they had been a soft touch. They hoped that by giving him a good deal they might get some business from his father's fleet. They were keen to expand their parochial little Norwegian ship insurance business from the co-operative it had been into an international one stop insurance shop for shipowners. He was quite happy to be headlined in their newsletter and on their website as an international client in return for a very good rate.

He had bought the ship in 2007 for $28 million. That seemed a good deal at the time. It was his way back into the shipping boom that would never stop, the one where so many of his contemporaries were making megabucks. But the global financial crash had changed all that, and today the ship was worth only $7 million. The daily hire he could get in the open market for the ship had fallen from $20,000 in 2007 to only $2,000 today. That didn't stop the bank hounding him for payments on the loan, he thought. They were only too nice to him when he wanted to borrow the money. His name on their books was good for them. Lately they had been threatening to force him to sell the ship, bankrupting CanDoTank. He thought it was a bluff to get his father to step in and bail him out. He didn't want that. His father was difficult enough as it was.

He thought the pirates had saved him. The ship was still insured for its original value. He should have changed that but had not wanted to reopen negotiations on the good rate he had got when he first came to the Club. So if the ship had to be abandoned and declared a Constructive Total Loss he would be paid $28 million. He laughed out loud. The best bit came next. The Scandinavian Club had also sold him loss of hire insurance. So when the ship could not deliver on its charter and the charterer stopped paying daily hire for the ship the Club would pay him the charter rate.

In this case the charter rate was $6,000 per day, three times the abnormally low market rate. Vexol did not find takers easily to move fuel to Al Shabab, and had to pay high to get a ship. But the charter was legitimate and the Scandinavian Club would have to pay six lovely thousand dollars every day while the ship was in captivity. If it stayed there for 180 days then it would be legally considered abandoned and declared a Constructive Total Loss. At which point he would get twenty-eight lovely million dollars. The Club would then own the ship and it would be their problem.

John C sat back in his chair. One hundred and eighty days. He had read of ships held much longer than that. He thought he could spin this out. Six thousand a day to keep the banks happy then all the capital repaid. It was perfect. He just had to keep the ship there. He thought he could do that. But he knew he had to look as if he was doing everything he could to free it.

* * *

The noise of the fans in the tennis domes made it hard to hear properly. The Hurlingham Club charged enough for its membership, thought Ellis. Then we have to play in this scruffy tent with fans whirring away. He was rummaging in his tennis bag for his notepad, phone clamped to one ear, making sorry-I-have-to-take-this faces to his partner.

"Mr Canopoulos," he said. "What can I do for you sir?"

His heart was pumping. Not from the tennis. It was all too easy to beat these office juniors. He only played them because it was a good way to impress them with his game and his club membership. And because the girls looked good in tennis shorts. He was excited because this could be his big break.

He brushed his blond mop back from his broad pink forehead. "That is kind of you to say so, Mr Canopoulos," he said. John Canopoulos was calling to congratulate him on how he had handled a charter claim, how good was that? "Piracy negotiations? Yes, sir, of course I can handle that," he said loudly. He was waving his right hand frantically at his tennis partner, making writing signs. Why didn't the silly girl bring him a pen? "Let me just take the details."

Ellis Davis had just been made a partner in a mid-size London Greek-owned law firm, GR Karagiorgis. It was known for chasing down every cent for Greek shipowners, whatever the merits of the case. The sharp Greek lawyer who had built up the firm knew his market. The business rested on stroking the egos of Greek shipowners and finding every angle on every case where a cent was to be made. That is why he had put together a stable of English lawyers with posh private school backgrounds and a constantly rotating bevy of good-looking mostly female assistants and trainees. The clients felt at home in this world and they pulled in the cash without shame.

Ellis was in full flow now, calling his people off the court. "John C has given us a plum," he told them, pushing his fringe back again. "Let's get the team moving. Diana, get me a new mobile phone with a new number, I'll need it just for this job. Letitia, Google up everything you can find on Somali pirates and ransoms. James, you get me all the guff on John C's current charter and the value of the *Prometheus*. Find out who he is insured with and who insures the cargo. God, it's good to be in action."

He grabbed his bag and strode off the court, baggy shorts swinging. He would not have been happy if he had turned and seen the looks the girls exchanged behind his back.

* * *

Jon Erik Wigand was rather pleased with himself. He looked out of his office window at the view of Oslo's fortress across the fjord. It had been a good move to come here from his native Gothenburg and take over the Scandinavian Club. His Swedish friends still teased him about living amongst the Norwegian barbarians. But that was the point. He had been able to bring them an international perspective. Open them up to the world.

Five years ago this was just a little co-operative

insurer of Norwegian shipowners, thought Jon Erik. I've changed all that. Got some real international owners in. Widened our offer. Pushed up the turnover. The Scandinavian Club is a force to be reckoned with in the international insurance world now. He was looking forward to his turn as chairman of IUMI, the International Union of Marine Insurance. That would come next year. Put us on the world stage, he thought.

His direct line rang. "John C, how the devil are you," he said. His Swedish friends also teased him about his Anglophilia. In his tweed jackets and cravats and on his eccentric old bicycle he was more of an English gentleman than the English, they said. He didn't mind the teasing. He felt at home with the English aristocracy. In his mind the non-domiciled London Greek shipowner community was high up the ladder of that aristocracy.

"A pirate hijack," he said. "How unfortunate, what a pity for you and the crew, of course. You can count on us, John C. You will have the full resources of the Club behind you."

He put the phone down. John C had assured him he had it all in hand. He would negotiate a ransom and get the ship out quickly. It would cost the Club a little, but perhaps it will enhance our reputation, he thought. The market will see that we stand by our owner when he is in trouble. No need for any specialist kidnap and ransom insurance. An owner can get all the insurance he needs with the Scandinavian Club. John C will speak well of us, and there is a big market to be won in the London Greek shipping community.

CHAPTER THIRTEEN

Things were looking up. John C wriggled in his leather office chair. The shipping press always liked his pronouncements. He was front page on the Lloyd's List website, top story on the Tradewinds website and spread across three of the four Greek shipping websites. He thought his public relations people had done a good job. Only perhaps his photo made him look a bit jowly?

"Leading shipowner condemns lack of action on piracy." The headlines were great. His PR girl Sue was a no nonsense blonde who knew the way shipping industry papers worked. "Canopoulos calls for piracy action." They all had the story of his tanker being hijacked. They had all the right quotes in there. Sue had understood exactly what he wanted to say. Why did shipowners pay tax if the navies couldn't protect their ships? It was the crews who mattered most. It was unfair on seafarers that nations did nothing to protect them. World trade would suffer if the piracy scourge was not stopped. He would work tirelessly to get his crew out safely. "Whatever it takes, says Canopoulos." Marvellous.

John C loved it. Working the press was so easy. Not one of the papers mentioned that the ship was registered in

Malta, which runs an ask-no-questions flag of convenience and where he paid no tax. Not one pointed out that Malta doesn't have a navy. None of the papers had troubled to check with the maritime authorities, who could have told them that at the time of the hijack the *Prometheus* had not registered its voyage with them and had not been using its AIS tracking system. Not one picked up on the cargo and its destination. Not one had anything to say on his track record as a shipowner, or the worse one of his father.

You look rich and you buy companies which the public can understand, like leisure clubs or an airline. That's all it takes, thought John C. Then they bend over for you. He wriggled again. Bending over made him think about the receptionist. Was it a coincidence that she wore those tiny shorts each time he came to the office? Only one hundred and seventy-nine days to go. With the piracy as an excuse he could put off flying to Greece to talk to his wife. With the insurance money he would not need to talk to her anyway.

He reached for his phone, then hesitated. Natasha? Or should he see how grateful the receptionist would be?

* * *

Jon Erik was a tall man. When he trained at the Swedish Club he had picked up the habit of working standing up at a high desk. The boss had done it and he liked to do what the boss did. It helped his posture, he told people. Made him look a little more naval, he thought privately. A bit special.

He looked again at the papers on his desk. The *Prometheus* was insured for $28 million. Surely not, it would only be worth a quarter of that, he thought. But that didn't matter, there would be no claim on the total value. The ship would be free long before the 180 days when a Constructive Total Loss would become an issue. What worried him more was the loss of hire insurance. It looked as if the Club was paying out $6,000 per day to John C.

Lucky man, in this market, he thought. He felt a twinge of doubt. John C was making all the right noises in the press. But there had been no call to say what action he was taking. Of course, the Club worked on a pay to get paid basis, the owner had to act then claim. But it was normal to discuss what you were doing with the Club and use their expertise.

He hesitated. If I call him now will he think I'm putting pressure on him? He pushed the doubt to the back of his mind. He's a top owner, thought Jon Erik. The Greeks care about their crews. He must be acting behind the scenes. They have their networks.

He reached for the phone. "Elisabeth," he asked his secretary. "Did you manage to track down any tickets for the polo at Cowdray Park next week? I thought perhaps I could fly over, invite John Canopoulos. Do a bit of marketing."

* * *

Ellis was speaking slowly and loudly. He always found that best with foreigners. He supposed these Johnnies in Somalia had some sort of a translator.

"My name is Ellis Davis," he brayed into his new mobile. "I represent Mr Canopoulos, the owner of the ship. I will be the only person you can talk to on this business, and only on this number. Is that quite clear?"

He thought the Johnny at the other end sounded Welsh. Like that bloody prop forward from Cardiff who was always trying to bugger him at school. Where the hell had this darky learnt his English? Did they have darkies in Wales? He wasn't sure.

"We are going to agree some code words," he said,

still enunciating loudly and slowly. "So that we are clear who we are speaking to each time. And I will have to take you through proof of life questions with the captain. We must be certain you have the crew and they are safe."

Ellis was getting exasperated. He hadn't expected the pirate to reply, "Look, mate, I can hear you, isn't it, we can talk anytime." He had read up about how negotiators worked. "Look, mate," didn't come into it. And Ellis hated Wales. All that pissing rain and those boring aunts who spoke with a clothes peg on their noses.

The call ground on. Ellis scribbled down that the pirate he was speaking to was called Abdi. He wanted $5 million. The crew were all safe. Ellis was very clear. The ship was not worth much more than $5 million so there was no way they would pay that. They would look at a payment of expenses for the pirates if they let the ship go now. Perhaps they could raise $500,000. Not a penny more.

Ellis put the phone down and looked up. He was hoping to see some admiration in the way Diana looked at him. She had been taking notes of the entire call on a wide yellow legal pad. "Not bad, eh, Diana," he said. "I think I showed them who's boss, eh?" Bloody girl could look a bit more enthusiastic.

* * *

John C could have chosen Holman Fenwick to negotiate this, thought Ellis. They've done more pirate ransoms than all the other lawyers put together. Or Ince & Co, they've done a lot. But he chose me. A man like that knows how to recognise a natural leader, he thought. This piracy business doesn't seem so tricky. No poring over detailed charter parties looking for clauses his client could claim on. This was real work for a man with his skills. This was his opportunity.

CHAPTER FOURTEEN

There were a few things Ellis did not know. He did not know that John C always took gullible people he wanted to impress to Annabel's. An evening in the Mayfair nightclub for the A list had been enough to clinch more than one deal. He did not know that the expensive-looking girls with Russian accents that John C had invited to their table had last week been entertaining the car lease finance people John C needed to back CanDoCars. And he did not know what it was like to work on a ship. Or to be held captive by armed pirates.

If he had known about the first two things he would still have enjoyed being there. He didn't care about the second two things.

Ellis thought it was jolly good of John C to bring him here. "A man to man discussion," John C had told him. "We can have a little fun as well." Ellis could feel the champagne in his stomach. He could feel the girl's leg opposite him. It was just touching his leg under the table. God, he thought, she's a scorcher.

He realised why John C wanted to talk to him

directly. John C had given him the key role. He was confiding in him. He could see what John C was getting at. Too right. The current market was shit, totally unfair on tanker owners. The charter rate he was on now was good. Those pompous Norwegian insurers could afford to pay loss of hire for a little longer. Norwegians got up Ellis's nose. So bloody righteous. Backwoodsmen with an oil well, he thought, that's all they are, almost jumping as the girl's leg accidentally brushed his a little harder as she sat up to take her drink.

As for the cargo, it was insured in France. What was all that about? Undercutting Lloyd's, he supposed. It was probably French companies that had cut the Lloyd's market down. Lloyd's had driven his papa mad with all those demands for payment.

I've got the message, thought Ellis. You can't say it out loud but it is good business to hold the ship there as long as possible. And we have to find a way to make both the insurers pay for the ransom. The crew will be fine, holiday in the sun for them. That bloody Welshman won't hurt them, thought Ellis. Poofs, all of them, all that singing and half the rugby team trying to get into each other's shorts.

He sat up and clapped John C on the shoulder. "I'm your man," he said, confidentially. He sat back, taking a long swig of the champagne. This is the life, he thought.

* * *

Pity John C had not been up for a spot of polo last week, thought Jon Erik. I could have had a little chat with him then. Makes this call a tad awkward.

"John C? Sorry to disturb you, old man," he said. "How are you? Lovely wife in good shape?"

John C did not seem to be in the mood for small talk. But Jon Erik knew he had to make his point.

"It's a bother, John C," he said. "I wouldn't normally disturb you when I know you will be tied up. I mean busy. But you know there is a Norwegian angle on this *Prometheus* business. The government here and the Norwegian Shipowners' Association have cottoned on that the ship is insured in Norway. I'm getting calls. They rather do want to know when we can expect to see the ship freed. Doesn't look good for Norway, don't you know."

He could tell that John C was put out. Perhaps it was a private moment. He could hear rustling in the background. John C insisted that matters were well in hand.

"Yes, John C," he answered. "I do understand you are doing all you can. I was wondering if you could give me a few details of that. A few pointers, a time schedule? Something I can mention if I get more calls?"

When the call was over he put the phone down and leant against his high desk. He had not got any pointers at all. Just a reassurance. It was all in hand. Was it?

He felt the doubt growing back. Surely John C was not stalling? He couldn't need the cash from the loss of hire that badly. It would only be a blip on his bank statement, thought Jon Erik. He looked out at the sunshine pixelating the windblown water of the Oslo fjord. That always cheered him up. Today it didn't seem to work.

* * *

Yusuf pulled himself heavily out of the skiff and over the ship's rail where it was lowest, close to the accommodation block. He felt tired and tense. He would be glad when the money came. These English were talking tough but they would pay. Then he could rest.

He walked silently across the deck. He saw the boys on guard slouched against the front of the ship's accommodation. The deck in front of them was a mess. He could see where they had butchered the goats on the mooring bollard. Blood and bones were mixed with chewed quat leaves in small piles. The boys did not get up. They did not show him respect.

He looked up at the bridge windows. He saw Abdi leaning there. Close next to him he saw the woman. Her head was uncovered and she was too close to Abdi. They were talking and laughing. They did not look down. They had not seen him.

Yusuf reached behind him and pulled his Kalashnikov to the front. He reached forward and took deliberate aim at the steel bulkhead just above the slouching boys.

The flat crack crack crack of the rifle mixed with the immediate whine of the ricochets. The slouching boys rolled clear and stood up, shouting. Yusuf did not look at them. He did not look up at Abdi. He was turning towards the bridge ladders as Abdi burst onto the deck.

"Talking to women is not your job, son," said Yusuf, quietly. He did not want the others to hear. "Your job is to guard the ship. Make these boys clean up. Set a proper list of jobs. Keep the ship in order and the boys alert. You are not at school now. Be careful of the woman. You will marry my daughter, remember that."

* * *

The blow came suddenly. Lisa felt a searing pain shoot up her back. The barrel of Abdi's Kalashnikov had smashed into her kidney. Yusuf had kicked the gun hard from behind, catching Abdi and Lisa by surprise.

She screamed, then cried out again as Yusuf pushed the gun a second time. On the phone she could hear her mother calling out, asking what was going on.

Yusuf had seemed too friendly. He had come with Abdi and with Abdi's help asked her if she would like to call home. Abdi explained that Yusuf wanted her to let her parents know she was all right. But she must also tell her parents to put pressure on the shipowner. "Yusuf says you will not be hurt, but you must tell them to make trouble with the government, trouble with the owner, get some cash out of them, isn't it.".

They had let her speak in Norwegian. Her mother was practical as always. Was she all right? Lisa tried to be calm. Yes she was OK. Yes she was safe. But the pirates wanted money and they wanted pressure on the owners.

It was an unreal conversation, as if Lisa was calling from any port on a normal voyage. But this was not normal. She was pregnant and she was stuck on a hostage ship. She could not stop herself.

"You have to do something quickly," she insisted. "I'm going to have a baby. I have to get out of here." Her voice was breaking. She felt Abdi behind her. He was holding the gun loosely against her. She thought he was only pretending to threaten her. That was when Yusuf kicked the rifle. He pushed the gun a second time then reached past to cut off the satphone.

.

CHAPTER FIFTEEN

Torild Aarberg had never wanted to be anyone except herself. At school she had been happily confident. She knew when she was 14 that one day she would marry Sven, the quiet, strong boy who would grow into a ship's captain, as his father had.

She was neat and clean and spoke directly. Working in the local hairdresser suited her and suited her clients. The local women could chat with her, but she never gossiped. Her confident touch as she worked on their hair was calming.

She and Sven had married in the local church in Ulsteinvik. Showers of rain had swept across the bay as they came out of the quiet, spare church. His long spells away at sea did not worry her. Together they had made a daughter. Torild had brought her up in her own image. Quiet, strong and sure of herself.

For the first time in her life she felt helpless. This should not be happening to her. This was for someone else. Their daughter was pregnant. She was trapped on a hijacked ship. And she had screamed down the phone.

Torild reached for Sven's hand. "We must do

something," she said. "We cannot just sit here. Lisa needs help."

She was looking at the shock on Sven's face. She needed his strength now. She saw the discipline coming back. She felt stronger.

"Yes, Sven," she said. "We can make a difference. We will start now with a campaign. The shipowners' association, the press, the unions, our neighbours, the government. We will make them all press on this shipowner and his insurance company. We will get Lisa home. With her baby. Our grandchild."

* * *

He had been looking forward to some press attention. Chairman-elect of IUMI, the successful head of a growing insurance business, the Swede who rescued an old Norwegian insurance club. He had imagined the interviews. He hadn't imagined these sort of interviews.

Jon Erik's phone had not stopped ringing all day. The first time he had answered it he had been intrigued. Margarite, from Aftenposten. He knew her vaguely. The shipping correspondent on Oslo's big afternoon paper. He had squared his shoulders, stood a little straighter. He was ready to give her his views on whatever she was calling about.

The first question had made him flinch. Did he know there was a Norwegian officer on the *Prometheus*? The second hit him like a punch in the stomach. Did he know that officer was a woman? The third question almost doubled him over. He felt faint for a moment. Did he know that Lisa Aarberg from Ulsteinvik, a 24 year old, was on the ship he insured, the hijacked ship that had been held already for a month? Did he know that Lisa was pregnant?

John C has really stitched me up, he thought. He

must have known. Why didn't he tell me? A small voice in the back of his head reminded him that he had not asked John C about the crew. Or was that outside his head, another of the torrent of questions he had tried to answer that day?

One call after another. It seemed as if Lisa's parents had alerted every newspaper, radio station and TV channel in Norway. As Norway has the most newspapers per head of population of any country in the world, that was a lot of calls.

It wasn't just the press. He had taken a call from the officers' union. Another from Gard, the biggest of the Norwegian shipowners' insurance clubs. They did not want to interfere but could they help? The competition, ringing to gloat, he thought. And then a call from Bergesen, the biggest Norwegian shipowner. He had been cultivating them for some time. They were just ringing to see how he was handling this. Reminding him that Lisa was trained by them and they saw her as one of theirs.

Jon Erik made up his mind. "Elisabeth," he said. "Please get Wikborg Rein on the line. That partner who helped us with the last difficult case. We need a strong lawyer now. After that I will take a call with John Canopoulos."

I'll get Norway's biggest law firm briefed, then I'll tell him we have to get moving, he thought. There is only one way out, a quick General Average agreement, and we can act and pay the ransom. I have to get that girl home.

* * *

"John C," he said. "Sorry to trouble you, old boy. But the shit has rather hit the fan over here. You do know that your second mate is a Norwegian girl, don't you? You know that she is pregnant?"

Jon Erik thought there was just a tiny hesitation before John C replied. He must know, he thought. These people care for their crews. It's part of their make-up.

"Her parents are causing quite a stir here," he went on. "All the press are onto it, and everyone in Norway is onto me. We have to do something to get her out, right away."

Jon Erik could feel the doubt growing inside him. John C did not seem to understand the problem. It was too late to say it was under control. He should be sitting here, thought Jon Erik. He would see just how out of control things can get when Norwegians get all wound up about one of theirs in trouble.

"Look, John C," he said, a little more forcefully. "I have no choice. I have to act. My preference is to take this over and do the ransom ourselves. But if you don't want that then at least you have to let our lawyers in on the negotiations. And we have to put in place General Average right now, so we can all act. I've appointed Wikborg Rein, and they will be in touch with your lawyer shortly. I hope you will encourage his speedy co-operation."

CHAPTER SIXTEEN

Diana is lucky, thought Ellis. She can learn a lot from watching me handle this case. Pity she is so uptight. He was moving casually towards the window of his office. Not because he wanted to look out. He wanted to get to where he could see Diana bending over to reach the lower files.

Lovely bottom, he thought. "Let's get the General Average correspondence all lined up, shall we, eh," he said breezily. "Have a look what the Frenchies and the whale eaters are proposing. John C is keen that we keep them on their toes."

Ellis went through the notes carefully with Diana. It was important that they sat side by side to look through her notes together.

The transcript of all the calls to Abdi was there. He was holding the line on the ransom amount, holding it well. Abdi was climbing down from five million. With each call he was asking a lower figure. He grated on Ellis. Ellis wished he wouldn't call him mate. The Welsh accent seemed to make it worse, why couldn't he learn English from Hollywood films like all the other darkies?

The French insurers were a doddle. So arrogant. They didn't want to contribute to General Average. The old maritime concept of all parties chipping in to save the venture doesn't mean much to the French, thought Ellis. They work on *sauve qui peut*. He laughed out loud at his cleverness. They were playing into John C's hands, irritating the Norwegians. You couldn't make it up.

What was Diana getting up for now? Couldn't the bloody girl sit still and concentrate? He wanted to go through the correspondence with the Scandinavian Club with her. The Club was being a bit tricky. Sentimental, he thought. All this about a woman on the ship. Amazons, those Norwegian women, probably shagging the captain or the boatswain anyway, thought Ellis.

"Diana, let's go through the Club policies and terms again," said Ellis. "We can find a few points to go back to them on. Calm their ardour, so to speak, eh. If they have their way John C will end up paying over the odds to get his ship back. Not good to let the pirates make a profit, is it? The Club is just trying to protect itself. They took the premium for the loss of hire insurance. Happy to take that, weren't they, eh? So now they can pay out a bit longer. It's our job to get John C the best deal. Now come and sit down, you need to concentrate. You can learn a lot here with me."

* * *

John C was bored. It was flattering to have this Lloyd's List journalist hanging on to his every word. He knew he had to do it. But she was a little on the plump side. Perhaps that would work in his favour, he thought. She probably doesn't get much interest from men.

"Penny," he said, smiling. "May I call you Penny? It's so good of you to spare some time to speak to a small shipowner like me. It's excellent that Lloyd's List shares my concern for our seafarers."

He was turning on the charm. He could see she was impressed by his invitation to meet him at the Ritz for tea. "Why don't we have a glass of champagne," he continued. "It so helps the tea, I feel."

His public relations people had briefed him carefully. Penny David was the new golden girl at Lloyd's List, the oldest newspaper serving the shipping industry. She was clever and ambitious, but could not quite hide that she thought shipping was a little boring. So she would be flattered to meet a shipowner who was a household name. In her mind leisure clubs were much more understandable than ships.

"There are two things that really anger me about the response of the government to piracy," he told Penny, leaning forward so his words would be captured properly by her tiny voice recorder. "They appear not to care about the crews. As a shipowner, that really hurts me. Our seafarers must always come first. Their safety and welfare have to top the list. That is why I want to speak out."

Penny was listening with attention. He thought he knew what she was thinking. With John Canopoulos on tape for an exclusive interview attacking the authorities over piracy she was guaranteed a front page story. He would make her day, he thought. Then tomorrow I'll see the paper and she will make mine.

"First of all, how can they be so careless of the security of our ships," said John C, looking Penny straight in the eye. "It is outrageous that nothing is being done to clean out this nest of pirates in Somalia. We have the US Navy, the Royal Navy and who knows what other navies parading around the area. They have helicopters but they don't do anything. Even if they catch pirates in the act of boarding a ship they simply let them go. It's not good enough and I demand, on behalf of all our seafarers, who put their lives at risk for world trade, that the navies act and act firmly."

He took a sip of champagne. So far, so predictable. What he wanted now was a little more tricky. He had to let the authorities know he was going to pay a ransom so they could stop him, without being too obvious.

"Penny," he said, confidentially. "You have to be a little careful with this. I don't want anything to go wrong in my efforts to free the *Prometheus* as quickly as possible. But the US and UK governments have got the whole ransom question wrong, quite wrong. They are trying to stop owners paying ransoms. They are tightening money laundering rules to stop us moving cash. They even link ransom payments to terrorist finance, how silly is that? If they cared about the seafarers like we do, they would know that money is not what motivates us. Paying a ransom hurts, but it is the only way to get our people back safely. The navy has let us down. The government should not stop us using our own money to ransom the ship and crew."

He thought he had pitched that just right. He was certain that the story would be splashed across the paper and website tomorrow, under a red Exclusive tag. Penny's cheeks were glowing slightly and she was looking around. She obviously liked that people were pointing him out. She enjoyed being the centre of his attention. He ate one of the tiny smoked salmon sandwiches and answered carefully while she asked him a couple more questions. How soon could he get rid of her now?

* * *

Abdi was knocking gently on her cabin door and calling her name. Lisa stood up stiffly. She made sure she was covered and opened the door a little.

"I've brought you some extra water to wash," he said. "Are you hurt? I did not want to hit you with the gun. I have found some painkillers."

Lisa tried to smile.

"That is kind. My back is very sore," she said. "Thank you, but I can't take painkillers."

As she said it she saw the understanding in Abdi's eyes.

"I heard you on the phone," he said. "You said *babyen*. You told your mam you are pregnant. That's right, isn't it? That's why you don't want pills."

Lisa kept her eyes on his. She nodded.

"Yes, I am going to have a baby. So it is more urgent for me to get out of here," she said, putting as much weight as she could on each word. "Please don't tell Yusuf. I don't want anyone to know. They will use it as leverage and blackmail." The she softened her tone and looked down. "Of course it will help if you are kind to me," she whispered.

She looked up again. Had she misjudged him? She saw his face break into a smile. She could see he liked her. In another place she might have fancied him herself. She kept her gaze on him. She heard him say it quietly as he turned away. Yes he would help her. Yes he would be kind to her.

She hoped he meant it.

CHAPTER SEVENTEEN

Jon Erik was in a bind. Bloody Greeks, he thought. I should have stuck to insuring Norwegians. But the Greeks have the money and the Greeks have the ships, so they are the people who need insurance, he thought. That's the bind. I need John C as my toehold in that market. I don't need the trouble this pirate hijack is causing. I especially don't need to be called every day by politicians and journalists asking what I am doing about getting this precious Norwegian girl home. Why the hell couldn't she be more careful, he thought.

He tapped on his desk. There was no way out of this one. He had to make John C understand that.

"Elisabeth," he called to his secretary. "Get hold of Mr Canopoulos and set up a lunch with him one day this week please. Don't take no for an answer. I can invite him to Claridge's, I know he likes that. Then book me a flight to get me there for that. And a room at that nice hotel opposite Harrods."

I'll tell him face to face, thought Jon Erik. My lawyers are getting no help from that young lawyer he has employed. He is almost wilfully obstructive. If we don't act now all our

Norwegian business will be finished. I'll give him a week and if he has not sorted the ransom by then the Club will act on its own. We will negotiate direct and ransom the girl. One week, I'll tell him. Then we act. This has gone on too long.

* * *

"Good morning, Mr Canopoulos," said the receptionist. There was only a slight emphasis on the word morning. "I have Mr Jon Erik Wigand of the Scandinavian Club on the line for you. "

John C thought that she knew very well that it was a good morning, because they had started the morning together in his apartment. Watching her dress in her hot pants to set out for the office had caused it to be a very late start in the office for both of them.

"Jon Erik," he boomed into the phone. "I have good news for you. My lawyers have agreed a ransom of one and a half million dollars. That seems a very reasonable settlement. I did say they were competent. I hope we can negotiate a contribution from the Club and from the cargo insurers. I have saved you both a lot of money."

Perhaps he had the wrong tone there, he thought. That girl was distracting him. "Jon Erik, I want you to know that the crew come first in this," he went on. "I'll get the money to the pirates as soon as possible, then send the ship to Mombasa to get the poor crew off and home. Your Norwegian officer will be back with her family within a week."

John C was aware that Jon Erik would try to organise the cash transfer direct from the Scandinavian Club. He moved quickly to forestall that. "I'm setting up the cash transfer from the Royal Bank of Scotland," he said. "They keep enough of my money and my father's money on deposit so it will be no problem. I have in mind a good security firm to arrange the delivery."

Jon Erik seemed happy, so he was able to say goodbye. "Perhaps a little shooting trip next time you are in the UK," dangled John C, before finishing the call.

That got the Club off his back. Now, how would he fix it so that RBS would stop him from making the pay-out? It must not come back to me, he thought.

He reached for the phone again. "Get me Ellis right now," he ordered. "Then I will need to speak to our relationship manager at RBS. That will take half an hour. After that I will need you to come into my office to help me. With some... paperwork."

Two calls, he thought. That will do the job. Then we will see about those hot pants again.

* * *

John C was a real wag, thought Ellis. He had mentioned that Penny David was "a little plump". Not so little, he thought. "Shall I get you a drink, Penny," he asked. They were standing on the edge of a crush outside a busy pub in Leadenhall Market. "Let me guess. A glass of chardonnay, large one?"

He elbowed his way back through the crush and handed Penny her beer. No wonder she's so fat, he thought, girls should stick to white wine. "It's all very confidential," he said, edging her gently away from the crowd. "I'm afraid I can't say anything at all about CanDoTank's business or the *Prometheus*. Things are at a tricky stage and any leak to the papers might upset the negotiations."

He had been confused by the call from John C that morning. Why did John C want him to do an interview with

Lloyd's List? To show we are acting, John C had said. Don't worry, my PR people will set it up. Just meet the girl, tell her you are a piracy expert, give her the big picture. Give her what she wants, ha ha. Make sure we come out of it as trying hard to get the ship out. Time someone tackled these stupid politicians who are trying to stop ransom payments. Time someone made it clear that paying to get a ship out is not paying terrorists.

Ellis thought he understood. He had never spoken to a journalist before. It was a pity the PR people had been so fierce about him insisting on them not printing his name. It would be good for his career. He cheered up. If I impress her now then she will come back to me later and I can get my name into the papers, he thought.

"Penny," he said. "I've read your articles on piracy and John Canopoulos. Very insightful. You can't quote me unfortunately, but there is a real issue coming up now for all owners. Something you might want to follow up. The British and US governments are tightening the screw on ransom payments. They won't allow any money to be paid if they think it is going to Al Shabab. It's a terrible situation that needs airing, for the sake of the crews. Imagine a hypothetical situation. A hijacked tanker, a ransom held in a big UK bank used by Greek shipowners by a reputable owner with a long-standing account there, pirates ready to release the ship, but because the bank fears they are linked to Al Shabab they won't let the cash go. That is an intolerable situation, don't you think? An owner paying his own money to save his crew is not money being paid to terrorists, surely?"

He took a sip of his gin and tonic while Penny scribbled notes. He thought he was quite good at this press stuff.

* * *

John C was working himself up into a lather. "Would you believe it, Jon Erik," he boomed down the phone. "Would you believe it! I ask for a paltry one and a half million of my own money to save my crew and those bloody fat, idle bankers sit here in London and refuse to give it to me."

He was ready for Jon Erik's suggestion. "You are of course quite right, Jon Erik. As always," he said. "The difficulty here is that even if you pay direct from the Club to the pirates it is still seen as coming from me. Royal Bank of Scotland was quite firm on this. The ship is now seen by the UK and US governments as possibly held by Al Shabab, which you know well is part of Al Qaeda. So any ransom paid to free it will be seen as money paid to a terrorist organisation. I could end up in a US jail for the rest of my life."

Jon Erik was pushing back. He was under intense pressure in Norway. They had to get the pregnant girl off. She was silly to get herself into the spot, but her parents were making a real fuss. John C sympathised with Jon Erik. "If these silly young girls kept their legs together it would make our job easier," he said. "I want to get the ship out as much as you do. But that article in Lloyd's List yesterday linking the hijack and ransom to Al Shabab has got the authorities climbing all over us and the bank. God knows where they got that rubbish from. The bloody newspapers are a real problem. The bank will simply not release our funds for a ransom."

"Don't worry, Jon Erik," he continued. "Give me a week or two and I will think of something. I'm sure we can find a way to get some free cash which is untraceable, especially if we can reduce the amount a little. It would help of course if you could speed up co-operation with Ellis and the French cargo insurers to get a General Average agreement. That would mean even less cash out of my accounts and make it easier to get round the money moving regulations."

John C put the phone down. That would put the insurers on the back foot. They would have to reach an agreement on cost sharing, which takes time. He knew Jon Erik wasn't happy. But this delay would buy him a couple more weeks. More even if Ellis played his part right. He could see the 180-day target now. Get there with the ship still in captivity and he would get his $28 million. After that Jon Erik could do as he pleased, it would be his ship.

He laughed to himself. He thought his fake indignation was rather good. As for that line about young girls keeping their legs closed, he had to laugh again.

He sat back. Now he had a problem. The ship could wait. He had to sort out his women. In Greece his wife obviously needed a good bedding. The receptionist had swapped her hot pants for a micro mini skirt today and had made a point of bending over to give him a good view when she brought in his coffee. She might have to wait, he thought. Natasha was getting sulky. He did not like sulky women, but she had a body and some tricks he wasn't yet ready to give up. So Natasha it had to be.

He picked up his keys and left the office. "If anyone calls I am at a lunch with investors," he said.

CHAPTER EIGHTEEN

The sudden clatter of helicopters startled all of them. Yusuf leapt to his feet. He was squatting by the camp. Talking with guards on the beach. Telling them the money was agreed and would come soon.

Away from the beach, closer in than the *Prometheus*, he could see two helicopters hovering over a French yacht which had been anchored there for four months. Yusuf knew there were three French crew on board, with four or five guards. His clan cousin had hijacked the yacht. Yusuf thought him stupid. There is no money in a yacht, no insurance to pay.

Now the French were here to get their people back. We will all pay, thought Yusuf. "Get away from the boats," he shouted. "Get away from the camp. Spread out. Lie flat by the cliffs. When they have their people they will come here."

The flat crack of single shots came across the water. Single controlled shots during a hostage rescue mean only one thing. That very highly skilled troops are in action. The pirates were getting French justice. One bullet each to the head.

Yusuf ran for cover, trying to get as far away as

possible from the boats drawn up out of the surf. He knew what would happen next. Lying flat behind a rock he squinted towards the camp and boats. He could hear the helicopters close. Then the whoosh of rockets. A boat went up in flames. A machine gun was chattering. The second helicopter was methodically stitching death through the camp and the boats, while the first hung to one side. Yusuf thought they were looking for movement. He willed his men to stay quiet. He thought that the French pilots would not know this was not the camp of the pirates who had hijacked the French yacht. He thought that even if they knew they would not care.

This was a rare chance for the French marines to hit back at the pirates. It would be justified later as a legitimate rescue and they would insist they had only fired on the camp after being fired upon.

The noise receded. Yusuf waited. No hurry to stand up and give them a target. I have to tighten up the security here, he thought. Find some more boats, and run this camp properly. We are too close to success to let an attack like this deflect us. In his heart he knew it would not be easy. The guards were already jumpy. They would be worse now. He could not afford to lose any more.

He stood. "Come on boys," he shouted. "They won't be back. We will get our money. No helicopters will come for our ship. I am not stupid enough to hijack French people."

* * *

Lisa braced herself. She could hear the satphone dialling. In a second her mother would answer. Behind her Lisa could hear Abdi breathing heavily. She felt him pushing the gun into her back. It was right on the bruise where Yusuf had hit her last time. She thought Abdi was trying hard not to hurt her. But she could feel Yusuf watching them. She could hear him speaking hard, flat Somali to Abdi. She knew what would happen when the phone was picked up.

It was her father's calm voice. Lisa tried to match it, speaking quickly in Norwegian.

"I'm safe. The pirates want to know when you will pay. They want money soon," she began.

"Engelish, beetch," Yusuf was swearing and pushing Abdi. "Speak Engelish. Send money now."

She tried but she could not stop herself. As the gun smashed into her kidney she cried out. She heard the hiss of her father's breath. She braced for the second blow. It didn't come. Yusuf had cut the phone call.

"Now you lose a friend, lady," she heard him say.

Abdi was holding the gun away from her. He looked crestfallen as Yusuf shouted at him and pointed to the shore. But he did not turn to look at her as he walked away. Lisa knew what had happened. Yusuf could see that Abdi was helping her. He could see that Abdi was interested in her. So he was being sent to work ashore. The one pirate who could understand her a little. A boy who seemed too nice for this. She had built some trust with him. Now she was on her own.

* * *

Abdi was guarding the camp. He hated it. It was better on the ship, he thought. No dust. Proper beds to sleep in. Each pirate used one of the crew cabins. All the crew had to sleep in the mess. Except Lisa.

Lisa, thought Abdi. That's what else I hate about this camp. Lisa is on the ship. She needs me to protect her. To help her. I'm stuck here.

He sat on the rock, his Kalashnikov casually across

his knees. He was used to the weapon now. He felt he had grown used to Lisa too. She speaks to me with such confidence, he thought. A woman like that doesn't depend on men. He had never met a woman like her before. His mother kept the house, kept the peace. She did what his father told her. His sisters rebelled. But only in small ways, he thought now. They will marry and follow their husbands. Lisa is different. She will be a partner. With a woman like that you can do anything.

"Abdi," he heard Yusuf growl. "Take the jeep and go to my house. The women want to speak of weddings with you. They need to know about your family in Cardiff. Go now, I will take your guard. I will not wait too long for you. You have to learn not to talk too much with women. Your place is here."

* * *

When Abdi came into the house the room was empty. They must have heard me arrive, he thought. Then he heard the shuffle of slippers. Amina's mother came in, head down, covered from head to toe as always. She passed him and stood by the door, looking out.

"You came alone, Abdi?" she asked.

Abdi nodded. "Yes, Mother, Yusuf says you want to talk of weddings. I have not much time. What can I do for you?"

He was conscious of movement behind him. When Amina's mother did not reply, he turned. He took a pace backwards. He could not believe his eyes.

"Yes, we want to talk of weddings, Abdi," said Amina, softly. "Do you think I will look good like this in Cardeef?"

He could not answer. Amina was wearing high heels, skin-tight jeans and a tight cashmere sweater. Her hair was down, thrown across one shoulder. She wore a tiny patterned scarf, which sparkled and set off her eyes. She does have a fantastic body, he thought. He felt a flicker in his groin. I'm going to marry her, he thought.

Behind him he could hear Amina's mother shaking with laughter. She would never have dressed herself like this. But Amina used expensive satellite internet connection time looking online at Italian fashion sites. She wanted her daughter to look her best. She wanted her son-in-law to want her daughter.

"You look fantastic," said Abdi. "You look like a model." Then he laughed. "My mam would have a fit if she saw you like that. My sisters have to go to their friends' houses so they can wear them clothes."

Amina had lowered her eyes. "You will be proud of your wife," she said, then slipped away.

CHAPTER NINETEEN

John C was at the head office of his CanDo chain of coffee shops when his mobile rang. He was glad of the excuse to step out of the meeting. Why couldn't these idiots make money? What was so difficult about selling fancy coffees? Starbucks made money, Costa made money. But each time he came here he was told CanDo couldn't. The market was down, or coffee was up, or they needed cash investment to outfit the shops with Wi-Fi. Why the hell should he give away Wi-Fi, he thought. Anyway I need the cash to launch CanDoCars.

He waited a second or two longer before swiping his finger over the smartphone. He was not sure he wanted to take this call. It was his cousin at Vexol. Vexol was none too happy at having its cargo hijacked. He could imagine that its relations with Al Shabab were bad. He had read only that day that Al Shabab was under pressure from Kenyan forces. They would be with no fuel for their pickups, thought John C.

It was bad news, he knew it. When he answered warily his cousin was jubilant. He had been told by Al Shabab that they would move to recapture the ship one day very soon. John C could relax on negotiations. Al Shabab would sort it out locally. They would kill the pirates, take the ship and cargo to Kismayo as planned and in a week John C would have his miserable ship back. And no, there would be no more lucrative charters for John C. Vexol would use owners who did not let their ships get snatched. Thank you and *kalispera*, regards to your wife.

John C felt his stomach twisting. He only needed a few more weeks. He had to get to the 180 days. Now these bandits were going to mess him up. He would get the ship back and not the $28 million he needed. It would be worth nothing in today's market, which was getting softer every day. He would have to sort out his wife for cash to launch CanDoCars. He would have to bankrupt CanDoTank to get the banks off his back. Or he would have to go to his father for money again. He would get a lecture from his father about how he had made money by careful timing when he bought and sold ships. How his son had done the opposite. It was not his fault, he thought.

He pulled his stomach in a little and smoothed down his tie. He would go back in and tell that wretched woman he had hired to run CanDoCoffee that she needed to sort her act out. He wanted to tell her that she would make a lot more money if she had a policy of employing pretty girls to serve in the shops. Something in her attitude told him that was not a good idea. She was probably a lesbian and a feminist, he thought.

* * *

Lisa was craving chocolate. Not any chocolate. She wanted a Mars bar. You could buy Mars bars at almost any seaman's mission. You could find them in every port in the world. Except the anchorage at Harardhere. Except when you were pregnant and stuck on a filthy ship with skinny nasty boys eyeing you up. Except when chocolate was only a small thing to ask for.

There was no-one she could ask. She could have asked Abdi. Now he was gone. She should have been more careful. More submissive. She should not have let Yusuf see her talking to Abdi. Now she was alone. Alone, but with a baby inside her. Alone except for a shipload of men, half of them armed and high on quat. And no way out.

Lisa began to curse CanDoTank. She cursed John Canopoulos. She cursed him and his family and his father and his businesses and his captain and his horrible little ship. With every curse she kicked hard against her bunk. She was sitting on her daybed, a settee that ran down one side of the cabin. Each kick against the wooden drawers under her bunk gave off a satisfying crash. She warmed to her task. She cursed Somalia, she cursed pirates, she cursed Yusuf. And as she cursed she kicked, feeling rage pushing out despair.

The cabin door shook as someone outside hit it with a rifle butt. "Woman!" she heard. "No noise. Sleep now!" Another crash against the door and silence.

Lisa felt all the rage and adrenalin drain out of her. She curled up and hugged her knees in tight. She began to cry, softly and quietly.

* * *

Yusuf handed Abdi a mobile phone. "Today we have good signal," he said. "Call your father. Tell him everything is good here. Tell him soon we will invite him for the wedding. Tell him his wife will need a new *dirac* soon."

Abdi felt as if he was calling another planet. He had left Cardiff only a few weeks ago. He had never seen a gun. Now he was a killer guarding a hijacked ship. It felt unreal.

"Mam," he shouted into the phone. "Mam, it's me, Abdi."

It was a bad line and he had to call back twice. His mother wanted to know what he thought of Amina. When would the wedding be? What was the delay? He could hear his sisters behind her, all talking at once. Ask him what she wears? Is she tall?

His father came on the line. "Son, there is a letter from your school. Your A-Level results, it says. Do you want to know or wait till you come home?"

Abdi thought his father had no idea what an A-Level was. No idea how important it was to Abdi. With A-Levels he would not have to drive a taxi. With A-Levels he could forget he had been a pirate. He would go to university. He would forget that he had worked in a halal butcher in a grotty shopping parade in the red brick ghetto where Cardiff keeps its poor and black people. His father knew none of this.

"Yes please, Father," he said politely. "Read them out."

When the call was over he sat quietly. He had what he needed to escape his father's life. A-Levels in maths, biology and physics. The grades would get him into Cardiff University. He had a new life ahead.

He looked up. Yusuf was watching him. First he had to escape this life, he thought. Should I marry Amina and be happy with a submissive Somali wife? Or should I go back to Cardiff? At the university there will be girls like Lisa. A wife like Lisa, he thought. That would be a different life.

CHAPTER TWENTY

The gunfire was close, raking the camp. Abdi rolled to one side. How had someone sneaked up on them? What had happened to the guard on the road? Next to him a boy he hardly knew was firing back into the dark. "Al Shabab coming," he shouted. "Shoot. They kill us all."

Abdi was thinking quickly. Al Shabab is a well-run military operation. They would not be attacking the camp just to kill a few pirates. They are here for the ship, he thought. They must have a boat. This is just a diversion.

He grabbed the boy's arm. "Come on," he shouted. "We will save the ship. Come on."

They crawled quickly away from the camp, then stood and ran towards the surf line. There was the skiff they used to take provisions to the ship. Abdi grabbed an RPG and a grenade from the heavier boat they had used for the pirate raid. He threw it into the skiff and together they pushed the boat out into the surf. Behind them Abdi could hear wild gunfire, but no-one was shooting at them.

The ship, he was thinking. Lisa is on the ship. Al Shabab will kill her. I have to save Lisa. The skiff was running now, the boy gunning the motor, glad to be free of the fire fight.

It took 15 minutes to get close to the ship. Abdi used the time to arm and prime the RPG. He knew what he was going to do. If Al Shabab came in a boat he would blow them out of the water.

Ahead he could see the dim lights of the ship. There, to one side, he saw the wake of a boat. It was closing on the ship. They must be only 50 yards away. He thought they slowed, hoping to surprise the guards. They would not have heard the gunfire out here. He touched the leg of the boy. "Slow," he said, waving him in a circle to come behind the other boat.

They will be looking at the ship, he thought. They won't be expecting us. They came up behind the other boat. It was close to the ship now. Abdi could see it clearly. Maybe nine or ten heads were showing. They were getting boarding ladders ready. He tapped the boy again. "Turn sideways and stop," he whispered.

He stood, bracing his knees against the side of the boat. It rocked in the swell and spray wet his knees. He lifted the RPG to his shoulder. The red light on the side was glowing. It was ready to fire. I don't want to kill these people, thought Abdi. If I go back now, they will live. But Lisa will not, the voice in his head said. He took aim at the centre of the boat. It was only feet from the ship now. He pressed the button. For a second nothing happened. Then there was a tearing flame beside and behind him. In front of him the boat exploded.

He tipped forward and dropped the RPG into the sea. Shit, he said, then ducked down again as the boy behind him fired his Kalashnikov. The boat he had hit had not sunk. Two men were firing at them. Then their guns stopped suddenly.

Behind and above them the guards on the *Prometheus* were firing down into the boat, finishing off the Al Shabab raiders.

It was over. He had killed again, but the ship was safe. Lisa was safe. Abdi bent over the side and was sick.

* * *

He was growling down the phone to Ellis. The idiot was agreeing with everything he said. Did he understand how important this all was to John C? Best if he doesn't, he thought.

"Al Shabab are getting shirty," John C told Ellis. "They tried to recapture the ship and failed. They have told my cousin that if he doesn't get the ship out and deliver the fuel they will go after him and his family in Athens. They may go after me in London."

John C was torn. He did not much care for his cousin, and thought him a fool to deal with dangerous people like Al Shabab. But he didn't want some Al Qaeda franchise turning up on his doorstep with a gun. If he wanted to he could get cash from his father and pay up now. That would take away the threat. On the other hand, if he could hold on for a few more weeks the ship would have been held over the 180 days and it would be a Constructive Total Loss. His cash problems would be solved.

He thought Al Qaeda was probably preferable to facing his wife and his father.

"Ellis," he continued. "We will settle, but first you must get the cash sum down to $1.25 million. Tell the Club that I am pushing you to settle with the pirates. Don't take any shit from them. Tell those greedy French cargo insurers that they have to cough up if they want their cargo out of there. Tell that bloody Welsh pirate that we are going to pay but he has to be reasonable. Spin him the money laundering story. Tell him the bank and the governments won't let the cash move. Let's get the ransom in place. But not too quickly. We should be aiming to get them out by, say, February."

It would be a lovely start to the year, he thought. Twenty-eight million lovely dollars. He could pay the banks off. He could tell his wife to fuck off. He could sack that bitch at CanDoCoffee. Get someone in with good legs. He just needed to keep his nerve and hang in there. He thought he could trust Ellis to get up everyone's noses for long enough to delay the ransom until after the ship was declared a Constructive Total Loss.

* * *

Yusuf hid his worry. "Abdi, you surprise me. You think quickly," he said loudly, laughing so the others could hear him. He slapped Abdi on the back. "You are a real man. You beat off Al Shabab. Your ship is safe. I think you want Amina too much."

He could see that Abdi was shaken. He thought he would be more afraid when he found out the truth. Four of the guards were missing. They had gone with the raiding party. That explained how Al Shabab had been able to get so close. They were traitors. When he had time he would find them and kill them. But now he had a bigger problem. There were too few of them to guard the ship and the camp properly.

"We will soon be paid, and paid well," he said. "Abdi, you saved the ship from those crazy Islamists. Now you will go back to the ship and guard it. We are close now to our money coming. Until then I will be here to guard, and Abdi will be on the ship."

He did not want to trust Abdi near that woman again. But he had no choice. There were not enough of them now.

He had to have someone from the family on the ship. Abdi had fought hard. He thought he must trust him.

He could see the boys looking around. He was glad when they began to question him. He could shout them down. They respected that. He could not succeed if they walked away.

He was shouting now, giving out orders, stabbing with his gun for emphasis. "And when you are all in the right places and doing your job then we can get the quat again," he said finally, his voice normal again. "While you argue like women the quat is waiting to be collected. Do you want Al Shabab to steal that too?"

* * *

Abdi was careful. He kept away from Lisa. He tried not to show her any favours. He did not want Yusuf sending him back ashore.

When he came back to the ship he had seen her. She looks tired, he thought. She needs help. He had asked all the crew in turn what they needed. Some cigarettes, some contact lens solution, some books in Polish, a call home, chocolate. He had sent the boat back ashore with a list. The list included Mars bars. For Lisa, he thought.

In Somalia there are very few shops. But anything can be bought if dollars are available. If dollars are not available then pirates holding a ship can buy on credit. Expensive credit, but they can get what they need. Two days later the skiff was back. Abdi went round the crew members again, handing each their request from the crumpled plastic rice sack which was faintly stencilled 'A gift from the people of America'. Father Christmas, he laughed to himself. He left the Mars bars until last.

She looks better, thought Abdi. It can't be just the

Mars Bars that have cheered her up. Lisa smiled and thanked him. Could she perhaps have a little more fresh water each day as well? To keep herself clean? She looked directly at him.

"You are a good man, Abdi," she said, then closed the cabin door in his face.

A good man, thought Abdi. A good man. She looks at me and sees a man. She is so strong, so confident. Not like Amina. Abdi felt uncomfortable. Amina was to be his wife. But he felt excited that Lisa had said he was a man. He would have to marry Amina. But he wanted to help Lisa. "Not just help, maybe," he said aloud. He looked around. No-one had heard him. He felt guilty.

CHAPTER TWENTY-ONE

What on earth could be going on, thought Jon Erik. He slowed his bicycle and stepped off it at the back of the crowd. Oslo is not a city of demonstrations. When they do happen they happen outside the parliament building or march along the Karl Johannes Gate. This crowd was blocking the Aker Brygge. Blocking Jon Erik's way to his office. He was late already. These bloody people weren't helping.

He could hear the chant now. "Lisa, Lisa! Open your wallet and free Lisa! Seafarers before profits! Bring Lisa home!" Most of the crowd were holding up pictures of a young woman. She looked pretty, with a big smile. I wonder what it is all about, he thought. All the shouting will make work difficult. I hope they get what they want and go.

Jon Erik was about to turn his bike and push through the thickening crowd towards the back entrance to his office when the crowd fell silent. Everyone was looking at a short, strong-looking woman who had climbed up onto a step ladder. She's right in front of my office, thought Jon Erik. She looks like the girl on the posters.

He almost dropped his bike. It was the mother. The

mother of that girl on the ship. She was speaking now. Her soft west Norwegian accent came clearly through the megaphone. "We are here only for one thing," she said. "To tell the Scandinavian Club that they must get our daughter Lisa away from the pirates who are holding her." Next to her was a dry, stony-faced man with grey hair. Must be her father, thought Jon Erik. And there are the press. There are the TV crews. It's me they are here for. It's part of the campaign. God, this has gone far enough.

He turned the bike and pulled up the collar of his jacket. As he rode off quickly he was cursing John Canopoulos under his breath.

* * *

Yusuf stood very close to Abdi. "Tell him to use *hawala*," he said. "Tell him *hawala* can move the money. The Engelish banks no good."

Abdi was on the satphone to Ellis. He thought Ellis would not know what *hawala* was. His family used Dashabilia, a local hawaladar who worked in the back of a grocer in Bute Street, to send money to the clan. They gave him money and his network paid it out in Somalia. All Somalis did that. But an English lawyer would not send money this way.

Yusuf was getting angry. "Tell him to send the money to Ah Hing. Tell him not to use banks. Tell him to go to Al-Barakat. They can move millions into Dubai. Ah Hing can move it to us. From Dubai everything easy."

Abdi passed on the instructions to Ellis. He could hear him writing it down laboriously. Abdi thought he did not take it seriously. A Malay Chinese in Dubai? A network of money brokers who worked on an honour system? They could bypass bank restrictions, really? Abdi could sense him sneering.

Yusuf was watching Abdi. He could see that he was not getting the replies he wanted. He pushed Abdi aside and grabbed the handset.

"Englishman, you listen," he shouted into the phone. "One week and I kill the woman. Two weeks and I kill the captain. No more wait. *Hawala* can bring money to Ah Hing, then money come here."

He gave the phone back to Abdi. "Make him understand. *Hawala*. Or we kill the woman."

* * *

Nikos Canopoulos was a nasty little man. He was known and feared throughout the international shipping industry. He had built up his fleet the hard way. First one old coaster which he captained. Then another, captained by his cousin. Then more and bigger ships. Scraping money together from his neighbours in the village. Cutting corners and cutting costs. Driving the hard bargains. He had got the timing right, buying ships cheap and running them cheap. Selling them when the market was high, then buying them back cheap when the market fell again. Today he had a fleet of 60 tankers. He was rich. None of that helped him. He would swap all those ships for a good son.

He could hear the captain's voice on the phone. He knew that the captain would not call him lightly. They came from the same village, but he was the big shipowner and the captain was still a captain. He had lent him to his son to captain the *Prometheus*. He hoped at least in that way his son would not cause too much damage with the ship. He did not want to get involved now. Every time he got involved with his son it cost him money. Worse than that, it made him ashamed.

"Captain, I understand," he said. "I know it is tough

but can you last out while John C negotiates? He says you will
be free soon."

The captain was explaining about the jumpy pirates,
the raid on the anchorage by the French and then the raid by
Al Shabab. He told him all the crew feared another raid and
more killing. He told Nikos about the arrogant English lawyer
who was upsetting everyone. He spoke in the soft Greek
accent of the Northern Sporades islands. He had been a good
servant to Mr Canopoulos for many decades. Their children
had played together. Could Mr Canopoulos not step in now
and help him?

Nikos was thinking. In his early days he had found a
couple of big insurance pay-outs very useful when his older
ships mysteriously sank at convenient times. But he had never
put his crews at risk. For him the crew came first. I put them
first and they go the extra mile for me, he thought. He had
guessed what John C was doing. Forcing a CTL. But it was
too long to wait. The boy was an idiot. And the captain was
telling him that the ransom was now only $1.25 million. He
thought his son spent that on silly women every year.

"Captain," he said. "You will be released. I will deal
with John C."

* * *

John C was holding the phone away from his ear. He
had heard this lecture on *philotimo* before. He could never
understand why his father cared about the ship's crews so
much. They got paid didn't they? Well paid, he thought, and
it comes out of my pocket.

"Yes, Papa," he agreed. "I understand. *Philotimo* is the
issue here, not money. We must of course be seen to stand by
our people and get them to safety. I have done all I can to
ensure they are safe and now I have reduced the ransom to

$1.25 million. With the Club and the cargo coming in we will pay very little."

He held the phone away again, a little further this time. Sometimes his father seemed to get angry for no reason. Wasn't he pleased that he had saved all that money on the ransom?

"Yes, Papa", he agreed again. "Yes, I understand. There will be no more delays. You will provide the cash and we will get it to the ship within a week. I will deal with the Club."

He held the phone away again. Was his father never happy?

"Yes, Papa," he said. "I'll come to Greece as soon as this is settled. I will respect my wife. Please give my love to Mama."

He put the phone down and groaned. The old fool would ruin him. He would have to ransom the ship.

CHAPTER TWENTY-TWO

A strenuous lunch hour with Natasha had brightened John C up. Someone appreciates me, he thought. I really gave her one today. She loves it.

"Get me Jon Erik," he said to the receptionist. Could she squeeze into even tighter shorts? Since he brought Natasha back into the picture he thought she was certainly trying. Despite the activities of the lunch hour he felt a slight tightening in his groin. She would get her reward tomorrow, he thought.

"Jon Erik, this has gone on long enough," he said. "I will not put up with any more delay. Our *philotimo* is at stake, our honour. So I am going to act. We will send the $1.25 million ransom to the pirates this week. I hope I can count on your co-operation."

Jon Erik seemed a bit put out. Well, tough for him, thought John C. He knows where this cash is coming from but he will never dare to say it to my face.

"I'm getting Ellis to arrange proper security with a reputable company for the cash transfer," he continued smoothly. "I trust we can rely on the Club to insure the cash in transit? You do want to play your part, don't you?"

John C was thinking that when the ship was safe he would get out of shipping. He would survive the blasting from his father and butter up his wife. She just needed a good seeing to and her cash would flow again. I won't need this silly little man any more. The receptionist could manage CanDoCars perhaps. She was a talented girl. She would be very grateful for a promotion.

"Yes, Jon Erik," he said. "I'll get Ellis to contact you with details of the cash transfer as soon as possible. Don't forget you must settle your part of the ransom and make the French pay out as well. This is General Average, not charity."

* * *

Was there life before Google? Yes, it was a stick in the mud life, all that jolly good fellow, who knows who crap, thought Ellis. Google cuts through all that. Lets the youngsters with a bit of go find the right people to do the job each time. Don't have to stick to the people someone else used. Dinosaurs don't understand how the internet opens up the market, he thought.

He was looking at websites for marine security firms. Plenty to choose from. APMS.com. Anti-Piracy for Merchant Ships, that had a great website. He clicked around. Looks as if it is run by ex-Royal Marines. That should stiff the darkies, he thought. Those Marine buggers don't mess about. Where were they based? Channel Islands? Clever, thought Ellis. Away from the tax man.

He glanced up and crooked his finger. "Diana, notes please," he said. He punched a number into the phone. "APMS? Good morning, can I speak to Duncan Jameson please? Your managing director?"

That sounded just right, he thought as he put the

phone down after the call. That Jameson chap was enthusiastic, no doubt. He had asked for a hundred thousand but had been quick enough to come down to fifty thousand dollars when Ellis had said the job was for John C. $50,000 didn't seem much for picking up $1.25 million in cash in Dubai and dropping it safely on the ship off Somalia. John C would be very pleased, he thought, and I'll charge the fifty grand to the General Average fund anyway.

"Got that, Diana, did you," he breezed. "You can always use a little leverage in this business, eh."

Why does she put that sour face on? Must be her period, he thought.

*　*　*

What was wrong with the woman? John C was being nice to his wife, but she was not playing ball. "Darling," he said. "There is no need to get worked up. Everything is in hand. I've beaten down the ransom to a level where my father feels he must pay up now. So I'll be sending the money off in the next couple of days. Then I'll be able to come to Greece. We can spend time together."

Perhaps she has got a lover, he thought. Why else would she react like that? Tell him to stay in London and keep out of her life? Why did she always have to bring up the subject of money? He had helped her invest, and she was married to a famous man. John C shook his head. Women, especially Greek women, were so irrational.

He tried again. "Darling," he cooed into the phone. "You don't mean that. I know my father has been silly and weak to do this, and it will cost me a lot of money. I mean he has really shafted a fantastic opportunity for me. But on the bright side it means we will be able to work together more. As soon as the cash is on the way and the ship is free I'll come to Greece. You are going to love the concept of CanDoCars. You can play a real role in that, we will make it work in Greece as well as the UK and across Europe."

Jon C winced. He didn't think it was anatomically possible to do what she had just suggested he should do with a CanDo car. He brightened. She obviously hasn't got a lover, he thought. She is just frustrated. Otherwise she wouldn't lash out like that. I can cure that and she'll be fine.

"Yes, darling," he answered. "Look forward to seeing you then." He realised he was speaking to a dead phone. Women, he thought, bloody hormones.

CHAPTER TWENTY-THREE

Lisa reached over the side rail and grabbed the rope thrown up by Abdi. He had come out from the shore. It was a calm day. There was only a low surf lapping the beach. She saw that his skiff was heavily loaded with drums of fuel and water and towing a second loaded boat. He smiled as he passed her up the painter for that one.

"Tie these boats up well, Lisa," he ordered firmly, but with a wry smile. "Yusuf says you will be towing us out to sea soon. Once we have the ransom money he will use the *Prometheus* as a mother ship to get right out into the shipping lanes. Then we take the boats and find another target and you will be on your way."

Lisa didn't reply.

"I do think the cash is coming tomorrow or the day after," he continued, to break the silence. "You will be safe then. I will be glad when I know you are safe. Promise you will call me as soon as you are home safe."

Lisa's heart was thumping. The money was coming. She was getting out of here. She was only half listening to Abdi now. Did he really think she was going to call him? She looked down at him in the skiff and saw his face. She realised he was serious. She looked around. No-one was watching. She smiled down at Abdi. "There will be a future for both of us," she said. She left him to work out what that might be.

* * *

In the APMS office in Jersey, Duncan Jameson was practising his clipped military accent. "Just a short task, out to Dubai, close protection, home in three days," he boomed. "No risk and three hundred a day plus expenses. Better than Afghan." He was talking to the mirror, psyching himself up.

A short and unhappy stint in the Royal Marines had ended on a misunderstanding. He had not had time to acquire any of the essentials of a good mercenary – a military bearing, a good group of loyal comrades and combat experience. But Royal Marines looks good on my website he thought. Now I have to phone these guys and get them to do the job. APMS.com was in business. Moving cash for John Canopoulos. It wasn't the first job that had come via the website. He had supplied a few Army boys as guards on ships. True, he thought, that hadn't gone too well. Two of the boys had jumped into the sea when an attack came. Muppets had to be rescued by a nearby frigate. Had to change the company name after that fiasco and set up a new website. This would be better. Moving cash would pose no problems.

There is an inglorious old boys network of which no-one wants to admit to being a member. It is all those who have left the UK and US armed forces in disgrace. RAF Regiment gunners who had sold weapons to the Taliban. Royal Marines who had a drug problem. Naval officers caught with their hand in the mess room kitty. US Airborne with post-traumatic stress disorder. Duncan kept up with the disgruntled and disgraced. He knew how these little misunderstandings hurt. But there was work for all of them. The war in Iraq was a bonanza for ex-military private security.

Afghanistan was good. But both suffered from one drawback. You might get hurt.

Somali piracy was much better. No risk really. Guards on ships lived an easy life, shot from above and rarely saw action. It was appealing to his people, and paid well. Cash transfer looked like being even easier and paying better.

"I'll call them later," he boomed to the mirror. "Action now." He pulled the keyboard towards him. Google could help him find a light plane in Dubai, he thought. Must be plenty of them willing to make a short flight over to Somalia and back. Not as if they had to land or anything risky.

* * *

The tall, dignified Arab straightened his crisp white dishdash and stood up to leave. He did not show it, but he despised this Asian bandit and these lazy European thugs. He was the principal of Al-Barakat, one of the best known *hawala* brokers in Dubai. The transfer of $1.25 million on a man's word was not a big deal. But he preferred to deal with honest men, not infidels.

The cash took up most of a pallet. Thick bundles of notes were tightly wrapped. They did not look well-travelled. He had counted them out of his vault only that morning. But the money had travelled a long way electronically before he had received the call from his cousin in Antwerp.

The money had begun its journey in a bank account Nikos Canopoulos used to help ease his oil business in Bulgaria. From there it had hummed along wires to a small bank in the Dutch Antilles. It had landed in the accounts of a company registered in Delaware, USA. Nikos had learnt long ago that all the best shell companies have US bases. From there it had moved with easy speed along more lines to the

Luxembourg account of a Liberian-registered trading company. A quiet, sober Belgian lawyer had given the bank the right codes, and the cash jumped into the account of a small, anonymous greengrocer in the back streets of Antwerp.

That greengrocer was the Arab's cousin. He was the main conduit of cash between most of the UAE and the Arab diaspora in Antwerp. Given the need of UAE women for lots of diamonds, it was a busy cash route. It was less usual for money to come back east, and his cousin and he were glad of it. But now it was done. *Hawala* had delivered the cash without trace to this Asian, and he would leave.

"You sit down. You go nowhere. We count money now," barked Ah Hing. He pointed at the two Europeans dressed in khaki shorts and shirts. "These men go to use money today. We do not want our friends to be disappointed."

CHAPTER TWENTY-FOUR

One and a quarter million dollars was a lot of cash. It took a lot more carrying around than either of Duncan's men had thought. Well, not quite one and a quarter now. It was only $1.15 million now. Bit less to carry. That Chinese hard man had taken his $100,000. Nasty piece of work. Duncan hadn't mentioned that when he booked them for the job. But then Duncan's briefing had been sketchy at best. They always were.

Neither man was fit. Bundling up all that cash and wrapping it in plastic had taken much longer than they expected. Getting it into the small plane was not easy and the pilot had not helped. They were supposed to be guards, they grumbled to each other. Close protection, not bloody porters. Could do with a fag, murder a cold beer. As for this crazy Russian pilot Duncan had found, hope he knows his way there. And back. Arrogant sod. Lazy sod.

They were in the air now, cooler at last, watching the arid land slip by underneath. Night was coming on. How long mate? Three hours to Djibouti, then we refuel. Wait a while for the daylight. The Russian did not waste words. One hour after that you drop.

Christ, three hours without a fag. Worse than the paras this was. The other man smiled slightly. Worse than the SAS, he said. Neither of them really wanted to know the true military history of the other. They both knew it was not either of those elite units. Best not to ask too much in this line of work. There weren't any good stories. They hunched down for the long flight.

* * *

Duncan was very pleased with himself. "Yes," he told Ellis. "It's all done. My boys just called in from Djibouti. They are on their way home. Positive eyeball on the target vessel, one pass and the cash dropped bingo right on the marker. They saw the pirates run and grab it."

"I hope Mr Canopoulos will think of APMS when he needs close protection for his next vessel transit," Duncan went on. "We only use good men, proven men, ex-special forces. Know when to hold their fire, not like the Russians. Know when to apply maximum force. Do it right first time. That's our motto."

"I'll pop the invoice over by email," he added. "Fuel and aircraft costs a bit higher than we thought but nothing too terrifying. Stay safe."

He put the phone down. He hoped Ellis would pay the account quickly. The damn Russian had ripped him off, mid-air blackmail once the cash was on board. Extra pay or no delivery. Muscle not much use in that situation. Guys on the spot a bit dozy. Had let the Chinaman skim off $100,000. Hope that was part of the plan.

Duncan was also thinking about a few cash flow problems closer to home. The company that had built his website was chasing him for cash, and the PR people whom he had employed to puff APMS to the press were threatening to tell the press he hadn't paid them. They were quite nasty about it. "You hired us to make you look good," they said. "We did that, now see what happens if you don't pay and we have to tell the press a different story." What sort of people were they, fancy PR, they could wait a month or two couldn't they?

* * *

The hot pants were gone this morning. Replaced by a short skirt. An extremely short skirt. John C thought he preferred the hot pants. On the other hand the skirt hid a promise. I wonder what she is wearing under it, he thought? He shifted in his chair as he felt the blood moving to his groin. All the business with the ship and the money was taking up time. He had been neglecting the receptionist. He was reaching for the phone, intending to put that right, when it rang.

"Mr Jon Erik for you, Mr Canopoulos," she said. "Would you like to be... connected?"

The minx, he thought. I'll give her connection in a moment. "Put him through then come to my office," he replied.

"Jon Erik, how can I help?" He was in full English gentleman mode. "I'm sure you are delighted that the cash is on its way."

The cheek of the man. He was questioning his security. Who did he think he was? He would whistle for any more CanDo business after this.

"Jon Erik," he replied, pushing his Charterhouse accent to the front. That man was a fool for the British gentleman act. "I can assure you, old boy, that the cash transfer is in the best of hands. We'll soon be cracking a bottle to celebrate the ship being released. It's a jolly good show all round."

He heard the office door open quietly and then close firmly. This call had gone on long enough. "Old boy," said John C. "You'll hear from the ship soon. We'll do a lunch. Have to go now – urgent business. Bye!"

She was sitting on the edge of his desk. He had to reach over her legs to put the phone down. God, perhaps she wasn't wearing anything under that skirt.

CHAPTER TWENTY-FIVE

It takes a long time to count one million dollars. It takes a long time to verify all the high denomination bills. They had the best technology. Better than most high street banks. They had a cash counting machine and a note verifier. Yusuf had sent them out in the boat the day before the cash was due. Somali pirates work together in loose networks. They share resources, and two things they share are a note counting machine and a hatred for counterfeit dollars.

Even with the machines it had taken hours. The plane had dropped the bundle in the early morning. Three boys kept a sharp lookout around the ship while the rest undid the waterproof wrapping. They stood closely around Abdi while he took each bundle in turn. Each pirate watched the others. No-one could be trusted when all those dollars were there for the taking.

Yusuf had told him to check and check carefully. Every note, every bundle, check and count. Yusuf sat to one side. Alone, aloof.

It didn't add up. There should be $1.25 million dollars. I've just passed A-Level maths, thought Abdi. I must be able to add this up. He went through the piles again. There was no doubt. The payment was $100,000 short.

The pirates were silent. They had been hoping to go home today. Some of them had been on their mobile phones, calling their families. He had heard one ordering a new jeep. One whispering, must be to a girl. They will be making a few more calls now, he thought. This ship is not going anywhere today.

Yusuf exploded. "The Engelish are dogs. They are thieves," he shouted. "They steal our money. They think we are fools."

"Call the Engelish lawyer, tell him we kill the girl first. Then we kill the captain. Then we kill all crew. Tell him they are thieves. We are honest men. We do as we promise. Get the money here in three days and the ship is free. No money, the girl is dead," Yusuf was still shouting. "Abdi, tell him, no money and the crew is dead."

Yusuf pointed his gun at the piles of money. "You and you, put all this back into one bundle. You will not move from it. When we pay out the money you will dance naked. If any money is gone you will dance for my bullets."

He has a real problem now, thought Abdi. He has to guard the ship from Al Shabab, guard one million dollars from other clans and pirates and guard the cash from our own boys. He was running up the ladders to the bridge. He wanted to get to the phone quickly. He did not know whether to believe Yusuf or not, but he did not want to see Lisa hurt or killed. They had to pay the rest of the cash quickly.

* * *

Lisa could hear Yusuf screaming at Abdi. They were right behind her, at the back of the bridge. She could hear Abdi on the phone. He was calm, but he was demanding more money. She felt her heart sink.

She had been on the bridge on watch when the plane dropped the cash. She had been looking down from the bridge at the foredeck while the cash was counted. As the pirates crowded around watching the count Lisa had been counting the minutes until the ship was released. She knew that Somali pirates always let ships go once they are paid. In her mind she was already in Mombasa port, already disembarking with her luggage, already on the plane back to Norway. Back to cleanliness and safety and good food and her mother and father and peace and quiet and Ole and a future for her baby.

But now she was back at anchor, and stuck there. Stuck in the heat. Stuck without running water. Stuck with nervous boys with guns watching her every move. She pushed one heel back into her other leg, hurting herself. It was her trick. She snapped herself out of despair. She straightened up, and looking aft caught Abdi's eyes on her.

He was the key to her escape. With his help she could take a boat and find a ship out at sea to rescue them. She knew he liked her. But would he risk everything to help her escape? She shook herself. It would not be easy. But she would make him want to help her. She smiled slightly and turned away. Her mind was made up.

* * *

Jon Erik could not believe what he was hearing. "I rather think we have done our part, old boy," John C told him. "If the ransom has come up $100,000 short that is hardly my problem. Honour amongst thieves and all that. They just need a little time to sort it out between themselves and they'll see reason."

Jon Erik had lost patience now. "You insisted on

appointing the security firm," he said forcefully. "We insured the transfer on that basis. Some gangster in Dubai has skimmed off money during the transfer. The payment was short of $100,000. My lawyers say that the pirates are angry. They may hurt the crew, especially Lisa Aarberg. What on earth were your security people doing? You have to make good the shortfall before something happens to the crew."

John C's voice on the phone sounded disdainful. "Quite to the point, I think, Jon Erik," he said. "Straight to the point. You Scandinavians are always so direct. You insured the payment. The payment is short. Therefore it follows that the shortfall has to come from you. The insurer. Couldn't be clearer, really. Don't you see?"

From his desk Jon Erik could look down through the window at the Aker Brygge below. The crowd was not there, but three people stood outside his office holding up placards with photos of Lisa. They had been there for weeks. He saw people strolling on the quayside stop and speak with them, then glance up at his window. This had to stop.

"John C, I'm sorry you are taking that line," he said. "We have tried to work with you every step of the way. Now the Club is going to act. I will arrange for the extra cash and organise the transfer. My lawyers will be in touch with yours. Who pays the money in the final settlement will be decided later. Today I'm going to get cash to the ship and get Lisa out."

CHAPTER TWENTY-SIX

Lisa spat on her fingers and reached down between her legs. She wanted to make this as easy as possible.

Tanker officers don't pack dressing gowns or seductive underwear when they join ships. Sensible ones do pack condoms, but Lisa thought she would have to take a chance on Abdi. It wasn't as if she could get pregnant. She wanted to make sure Abdi got the message, but she didn't want to frighten him or put him off. So she was wearing pyjamas and she was thinking how she could slip out of them without being too obvious. She had washed herself as well as she could and brushed her hair back. She didn't think she would stand much chance of getting a boy in an Oslo nightclub. But she was going to do her best to get Abdi, and she wanted Abdi to believe she was a woman worth getting.

She switched off the light and left the door half open. She was tense, too tense. In Lisa's life sex was simple. If she liked a boy and felt like sex, then there was always a way. But if she did not feel like it or did not like the boy, then there was no sex. She had never played games. Never had to compromise. Never thought to use sex as a way to get what she wanted. Until now.

She heard Abdi coming. He walked quietly, more hesitantly than the other pirates. "Lisa, you must keep the door shut," she heard. Then she reached her hand out to find his. "I'll close it if you come in here with me," she said softly.

Abdi stepped over the storm sill into the cabin. Lisa could see the look on his face. She was touching his hand and suddenly it was all going to be easy. She reached behind him to lock the door.

* * *

Abdi was leaning against the bulwark. He was looking out to sea, but he would not have seen any ship that sailed past. All he could see was Lisa.

He was glad of the bulwark. He was trying to hide his erection. He felt ashamed that his shorts were bulging, but he could feel the tightness and heat across his groin. He almost felt sick and looked around sharply. Had he groaned out loud?

Down on the deck the day's business went on. The cook was slaughtering a goat. The mate was doing something forward with the anchor windlass, probably hoping that soon he would be heaving up the anchor and leaving. There was no sign of Lisa, and no-one was paying him any attention.

One hand touched his shorts. He thought he was going to come. Last night Lisa had guided him gently into her. She had told him how good and strong he was. He felt her hands pulling his body onto hers. He could feel the softness of her breasts and the hard muscular body that had moved under him.

It had been dark. He wanted to see her. It had been too quick. He wanted to be with her again. To have time to look at her. To feel her pulling him inside her.

He did not feel any shame, only desire. Lisa was modest when in company, but direct and sure of herself. In the darkness of her cabin she had also been sure of herself. But welcoming, hot, wanting him. He wanted her. Not a woman who was submissive. Not a woman who played games. A woman who was strong and capable. He wanted Lisa.

Abdi was daydreaming now. When the final cash instalment came Lisa could go free. He would find a way to escape Somalia. He would not marry Amina. He would be free of pirates, free of his past. Lisa would be waiting for him. They would live together, run a business together. And at night she would be his.

Yusuf's barking voice brought him back sharply. He was shinning up a ladder from a skiff, already rapping out orders as he came on board over the rail. Abdi was careful not to move too quickly, relieved that his erection was subsiding.

"Father, I'm listening," he said. He checked his shorts and made his way to join the other pirates who were grouping round Yusuf.

* * *

Jon Erik was sitting down, holding his head in his hands. He did not feel like the tall, confident Swede who had come to Oslo to invigorate an old Norwegian shipowners' insurance club. He felt like a failure. He wasn't used to feeling like that.

At least it would all be over soon, he thought. In a long session of calls he had spoken with all the key players in turn. First the most experienced London piracy lawyers, Holman Fenwick. A specific plan and a timetable please. What had been done up until now? He felt ashamed when he heard the reaction to the name of the security firm John C had employed. How had he allowed himself to be fooled?

The second call was to DNB, Norway's main shipping bank. They handled the Club funds. It was no problem to produce $100,000 in Nairobi tomorrow. They were happy to be helping to free Lisa Aarberg. They didn't say it was a pity he had not acted before. They did not need to. Their tone of voice was enough.

The third call was to the security firm Holman Fenwick had recommended. Yes, they could guarantee delivery to the ship tomorrow. Glad to be of assistance sir, especially in this case. Understand there is a pregnant woman involved. Not so good, but we'll get the cash to the right place, you can rely on that.

The fourth call was to his lawyer at Wikborg Rein. Yes, they would take over the negotiation and deal with Holman Fenwick. Cut out John C's English lawyer. Of course things would move more quickly like that. Glad to help Lisa. And we will brief you on all the options for recovery of the cash from CanDoTank once the ship is free.

Jon Erik thought he was screwed both ways. He had to attack John C now to get the Club's money back. He would get no more business from London Greeks. Where would the business come from? Not from Norway. He was a hate figure here now. Today his underwriting director had come to him. The Club was bleeding business. Norwegian owners were deserting them. Only the cheapest were renewing, and only then when they could screw the premium down to rock bottom.

Bloody pirates, he thought. Bloody Greeks. Bloody woman. Bloody, bloody village Norwegians. Why did I ever come here?

CHAPTER TWENTY-SEVEN

Yusuf felt good. He looked around the ship. It was tidy and the guards were alert. He had enough cash already to pay Ah Hing and the boys, and he knew that he would soon have more.

The boys were fired up. Seeing the cash counted had changed their attitude. Word gets round quickly. More boys were turning up, looking for a job. His phone was ringing with offers of investment. He thought he would take advantage. The weather was good. One more strike would make this a real wedding.

Yusuf walked aft and looked over the stern of the ship. The skiffs were fuelled up and ready to go. He had the boys, he could find new guards while he was away. Tonight was the end of Ramadan. There would be a feast. Tomorrow everyone would be hung over. But they could eat and drink and Allah would not mind if they did a little more coastguard work during the day.

"Listen," he shouted. "Listen to me. Tonight is the beginning of Eid al-Fitr. Al Shabab will feast for three days. We will party only tonight. Tomorrow we will go to sea again.

It will be quiet. The Islamists will sleep and our ship is safe. The cash will come soon. While we wait we can take another ship. The foreigners get lazy during Ramadan. They believe that all Somalia is praying and fasting. I need six of you. Six who will come with Abdi and me. The boats are ready. The weather is good. In two days we can have another ship here at anchor. Who will come with me?"

For a moment there was silence. Then the boys began talking quickly to each other. They had enough already. No, I need money to marry. My Toyota is already broken. That woman in Mogadishu is waiting for me. What about our families?

Yusuf knew he had them. One boy stood forward. "If I can go tonight to my family home for the first night of Eid I will be back here tomorrow and will be the first to board the ship," he said. Behind him the others clamoured to speak.

"Enough," Yusuf shouted. "Tonight you go to your families. I have boys waiting to take over as guards. Tomorrow you return and we go hunting."

He turned to look at Abdi. "Tonight we will eat at my house," he said. "Tonight you will share a table with Amina. We will fix the wedding date. Tomorrow we go again and *Inshallah* we will become rich. God is good."

* * *

Lisa could feel Abdi watching her. She was careful to keep to her routine. She dressed as always in overalls, covered her hair, and now she was halfway through her bridge watch. Each of the officers took turns to be in charge at the anchorage. They did not expect anything to happen, but the captain saw that the pirates were not seamen and he wanted one of his officers alert at all times. A change of weather could see them dragging the anchor and beaching the ship.

He did not want that to happen when release was so close.

She stood inside the bridge door, trying to look casual. Her stomach was churning. Last night he had been happy, a young boy becoming a man. And to her surprise she had enjoyed the sex. She had let herself go and thought he could have been any other boy on a summer's night. But would he feel shame now? Would he hate her? She needed him to want her, not just for sex, but for the future.

Abdi was on the bridge wing. She could feel the tension in him.

"Abdi," she whispered. "Abdi. Abdi. It is good to see you."

She thought he relaxed. He was leaning on the bridge wing now, keeping his body turned away from her, but looking at her. He spoke quickly and urgently. Lisa. He wanted her. Lisa. He wanted to escape from Somalia. He wanted to live with her. Lisa. He wanted to build a business with her. Lisa. Lisa. Lisa.

Lisa knew she could not touch him or go close to him. There were too many eyes around the small ship. But in the shelter of the bridge she loosened the top buttons of her overall and leant forwards towards him when she spoke. She saw his eyes flick downwards and widen slightly. She felt a surge of pride, a flood of relief. She stifled a giggle. She could guess why he had his body pressed forward against the bridge wing front and away from her.

"Abdi." Her voice was a little stronger now, but no-one outside the bridge would have heard it. "Abdi. You are a good man. This is not your place. We can do this together. We don't need to wait for the payment. You don't need to escape alone. We can do this together. The boats are there, fuelled and ready to go. I can work the outboard motor. I can navigate. I can find a ship to rescue us. Together. Together, Abdi. Tonight."

She saw his surprise. It was too sudden. She thought if she could just touch him now, it would be done. But she could not. So she stood, simple, strong, a woman, and waited. He looked up. His eyes were shining.

"Tonight Yusuf has ordered a feast for the end of Ramadan," he said. "Tonight everyone will be distracted. I will have to be with Amina and Yusuf, but I will tell them I have to check the ship and guards first. If I give them drink we can do it then. Tonight, after dusk."

Lisa felt the relief flowing through her. "Tonight," she breathed. "Yes Abdi. Tonight. Tonight we start our new life. I'll be ready."

* * *

Abdi felt natural in his role as Yusuf's second in command. Somalis don't respect authority, but they respect family links and they respect power. They also respect people they have seen kill. So Abdi had status in their eyes. Soon he would be Yusuf's son. He would have money and be tied by marriage to the big man. He had killed. Killed to take the ship, and killed to save the ship from Al Shabab.

His Somali still sounded strange to them. He had tried to explain where Wales was, where he came from, but Engeland was as far as he could get in making them understand. But now as he spoke they were all listening intently. He had just come on board, swinging easily up the ladder with a clinking bag on his back. "Tonight we can celebrate," he told them. "We celebrate the end of Ramadan. Tonight Yusuf is busy with his women and food and drink. So I have brought drink for us too. Ethiopian gin. It is what Yusuf drinks. And quat, good quat from Kenya. The ship is safe, we can enjoy ourselves. I will have to go back to the old man and the women, but first I will drink with you."

He had called them all together on the foredeck, in the shelter of the accommodation. They were careful to keep the cash in sight. No-one could be alone with the cash. They sprawled on the mats spread on the deck, chewing, spitting, and drinking from the bottles Abdi passed around. He drank with them, but always from his own bottle. He was waiting for night to set in, and he had made sure his bottle contained only water. He wanted a clear head for later.

CHAPTER TWENTY-EIGHT

Lisa could almost see the funny side of it. All the struggle to keep clean with only jugs of water to wash with, and now she was smearing dirt on her face. She had raided the engine room rag stores for a black cloth to wrap her head in. She looked in the mirror. The dark figure in the dirty overall, grimy face and black rag wrapped around its head was not Lisa. Was not a blonde young woman. It was someone who could slip unnoticed into a boat at night.

She tensed as the door was opened slightly, then relaxed as Abdi's hand reached in to click the light off.

"Lisa, come, we can go now," he spoke, softly, sounding surprisingly calm.

As they moved quietly along beside the accommodation to the after deck they could hear the guards on the foredeck. The Ethiopian gin combined with the quat was making them noisy. Abdi could hear them boasting of what they would spend their share of the ransom on. He slowed as he listened, then began to move more quickly as Lisa's hand found his in the darkness.

The two skiffs were bobbing quietly behind the ship,

lying back in the light wind, tugging on their painters. Lisa pulled one in hand over hand and gave Abdi a light push. "Jump down into the boat, Abdi," she said. "I've got it."

Abdi landed clumsily then almost cried out as Lisa bundled down on top of him. He felt her breasts crush against him through the overalls. She was whispering in his ear. "Find the paddles, Abdi. We have to paddle clear before we start the engine."

Lisa slipped the painter and the skiff drifted away from the ship, carried by the breeze. She had her hand on Abdi's, urging him to paddle quietly, get them some safe distance in the darkness.

When the ship was a low glow in the distance she turned to the outboard. Lisa knew outboards. She felt for the kill cord, felt again to check the fuel was on and air feed open. She pressed the starter. Nothing. Again. Nothing. She could feel rage rising. Why do fucking outboards always let you down when you need them most?

Abdi was reaching past her. "There is a switch," he said. He was still whispering, although they were too far for anyone to hear them. "Yusuf has another switch, to save the batteries, he told me."

She heard the solid click of the isolator switch, then hit the starter again. The motor purred into life. Lisa thought she felt the baby kick. They were on their way home.

* * *

Lisa set the outboard at three-quarters throttle and moved aside to let Abdi steer. She leaned into him and pointed the way ahead. "Head for that star, Abdi," she whispered. "That star will take us away from the shore. Now I will find a ship to take us to safety."

Lisa knew AIS systems backwards. As an officer on merchant ships she used AIS every watch, and checked it frequently. This set looked just like several she had sailed with. She thought it had probably been stolen from another hijacked ship. Abdi touched her arm, guiding her hand to a torch. She saw quickly how Yusuf connected the big boat battery. Two quick twists of the wires on the terminals and the screen sprang into brightness. She went through the standard setup. Receiver on. Transponder on. Link to GPS on. And then she selected the longest range scale. Somewhere out there was the ship that would get her out of this mess.

Lisa rested her back against Abdi's legs. On her lap were the GPS and AIS. She was watching the GPS to make sure Abdi kept a good course directly away from the coast. She was watching the AIS because she knew that after three hours at this speed they would be far enough from the coast to find shipping. And she kept her back touching Abdi's legs because she wanted him to feel her body. She did not want to take a chance on him changing his mind.

She did not know what she would do about Abdi once they were rescued. He was a nice boy. She had taken him into her bed and enjoyed it. But he was also one of the pirates who had captured her. And he could have no part in her future. She shook her head. First they must get rescued, then she would worry about Abdi.

Half dozing, she missed the first trace. Then it painted on the screen again. *USNS Manitowoc.* An American ship. Forty miles away and moving slowly North North West. The screen updated again. There was no mistake. It was a US-flag tanker, moving at only eight knots. The AIS did its job. The ship was 206 metres long and carrying 31,000 tonnes of oil, bound for Bahrain. To her seaman's eye it didn't make sense. The ship was moving too slowly and was not on course for Bahrain. But to her desperate mind it made a lot of sense. It was an American ship. They could catch it, and it would rescue them.

She reached behind her, squeezing Abdi's leg. "Here we go," she shouted, pointing at the AIS screen. "Come this way, turn the boat to point there. And go full speed. In three hours we will be safe."

CHAPTER TWENTY-NINE

Alan T Garcia had been a United States Merchant Marine captain for a long time. He'd seen it all, been everywhere and was proud of his career. He was proudest of all now as master of the *USNS Manitowoc*. She was a fleet oiler, a civilian ship run by the US Military Sealift Command, dedicated to keeping the world's biggest and best Navy functioning. Wherever the US Navy went, ships from the Military Sealift Command went too. Or more often, were there first. They carried the fuel that kept the ships running, the jet fuel that kept the fighters flying from the carriers, the shells and rockets and bombs that the Navy needed to do its work, and the food that hungry Navy boys needed to keep them working.

Captain Garcia was proud because the US Navy depended on his civilian-manned ship performing, and perform it always did. Now on a war footing he had a small Navy detachment embarked for protection. A young lieutenant and three sailors who manned two 0.50 calibre machine guns. But the ship was run by the Merchant Marine, and he made sure it ran properly.

They were idling slowly northwards ready to refuel

and replenish a US frigate that was on its way back to its regular station in the Gulf of Aden. The frigate had been out in the Indian Ocean, trying to locate a reported pirate mother ship. Now it needed to refuel, and in a few hours it would range up alongside *USNS Manitowoc*. Hoses would swing across the seas between them, and fuel would be pumped in, keeping the fighting ship at 80 per cent topped up. Ready for action. Captain Garcia's job now was simple. He had to have his ship in the right place, and to stay safe.

He was dozing on his day bed when he heard the bridge intercom. "Captain, you should be up here. We have a small fast craft closing." He missed the second sentence as he moved quickly to the door of the sea cabin. Just the first sentence was enough.

On the bridge the watch officer was puzzled. He pointed to the AIS. "On there you can see this unit, Cap'n" he said. "It says it is a Ukrainian ro-ro ship, name of *Fanja*, bound for Djibouti. But it is moving at 25 knots and it is coming straight for us. And although it is only 10 miles away I don't see any lights or anything on the radar. I never heard of a 25 knot ro-ro ship and we ain't any place near the course for Djibouti."

Captain Garcia looked at his watch. It was coming up to 0500, dawn light. He stepped out onto the bridge wing and lifted his binoculars to scan the horizon along the bearing of the target. "Call him on the VHF," he said. "Ask him why he is not showing any lights. And tell the guy to keep clear. We are on Navy business. US Navy business. And wake that lieutenant and his boys. We might just need the .50 cals."

* * *

Lisa was holding tight to Abdi's legs now, squeezing herself to him. She was going to make it. The ship was close now. If she stood up she would see it. She could see the welcoming smiles. She knew her mother would cry softly. She laughed to herself thinking of her father. He would not cry, but she would know from his face that he was happy. She would be safe and clean and the baby would be safe and she would be meeting Ole and she could tell him about the baby and plan for the future.

The engine was screaming at full throttle, slamming the boat over the waves. Then the engine coughed, hesitated. It caught again but as she turned to see what Abdi was doing she heard it die. The boat slowed suddenly, throwing her painfully forward. The boat went quiet. No wind noise, no engine. Abdi was looking stunned.

Lisa knew boats, and she knew that outboards always let you down at the critical moment. "It's the fuel, Abdi," she said quietly. She didn't want to panic him. "It's only the fuel tank is empty. Look, we have fuel in these drums. You told me that. We put some into the tank and we will catch the ship."

Abdi did not respond. He was not looking at her. He was not looking at the engine. He was standing looking away behind the boat. Lisa saw him tense up and heard him. "It's Yusuf, man," he said. "He's chasing us. See! That's him innit?" He was pointing into the half-light. Lisa looked along his arm. She could see a black dot and a white bow wave. She felt as if she had been punched in the stomach.

"We can do it," she said, forcefully. She was shaking Abdi. "You and I, we can do it. Grab the fuel can and we are off." She was tearing the top from the fuel tank, and Abdi sprang into action, helping her pour fuel from the jerry can into the tank. Fuel was splashing down the tank sides as more went outside the tank than in, but Lisa knew she only needed a few litres.

"Let's go," she shouted, firing up the engine. Ahead

now she could see the bulk of the grey ship, moving steadily away. Behind them and closing fast she could see the other skiff. There was only one figure visible in it. She did not have time to think about how Yusuf had found them in the open sea. She was holding Abdi's left hand, and with his right hand he was steering towards the ship, with the engine on maximum power. Lisa thought he had made his choice.

Her hand tightened on Abdi's. The engine was shaking and roaring at full power. "They've seen us," she screamed. "They've seen us." Behind them the skiff was only closing slowly. Ahead the ship was flashing a bright white light at them, and they could hear the ship's siren blowing. The ship would wait for them, and they would get there before Yusuf could get near enough to threaten them. He would not get near enough to shoot, or near enough to make Abdi doubt.

On the bridge of the *USNS Manitowoc* Captain Garcia had only one thought in his head. He and his crew were sitting on top of a ship full of fuel and ammunition. He did not want to be another *USS Cole*, struck by a suicide bomber in a high-speed boat. It would be one big bang.

"Get the crew to general quarters," he ordered the officer of the watch. "Lootenant," he turned to the Navy officer hovering behind him. "Your boys can warm their guns up." He could see clearly now that there was a skiff heading for them, and that it had slowed or stopped. The office of the watch was pointing further out at a second skiff coming up fast. "He's waiting for his friends, Cap'n," he said.

The first skiff speeded up again. Captain Garcia went by the book. "He's not on the radio," he said. "Flash him with the big signal light. And give him the horn. He might still be some dumb fishing boat."

From the bridge their binoculars could see into the

first skiff now as it lifted on the waves. Captain Garcia could make out two figures and a lot of drums and packages. That didn't look like any pirate boat set on boarding, but it didn't look like a fishing boat. It looked horribly like a suicide bomber. And it didn't look as if the flashing light or horn blasts were going to make it turn away. "I guess we ain't expecting any visitors, Lootenant," he said. "Get your boys to stop him. He's had his chances."

The US Navy has well-polished words of command. They have been thought out and honed down the years. Drilled into gun crews and gun fire directors. Used correctly they eliminate misunderstandings. They make sure lethal force is only used on the right targets at the right time. But when US Navy officers think they are about to become the target of a suicide bomber they don't always stick by the drills.

The lieutenant shouted to the port side gunner. He was pointing at the first skiff. "Hit that motherfucker," he screamed. "Take the fucker out."

CHAPTER THIRTY

Lisa saw the flash of the gunfire on the ship at the same time as she saw the spouts of water stitching towards them. She felt the bullets thud into the boat. Abdi's hand was torn from her and she saw the engine casing shatter.

"It's us!" she was shouting. "You need to shoot the other boat. I am a Norwegian, a woman." She was not thinking. No-one could hear her. She thought that if she stood up they would see she was a woman, and would come to rescue her.

She stood, bracing herself, and looking at the ship waved her arms above her head.

The sailor manning the portside machine gun was a big milk-fed farm boy from Wisconsin. He had a simple view of the world. He wasn't going to mess with anyone. Just so long as they didn't mess with him.

Looking down the sights he could see he had hit the boat and stopped it. He thought he had done a good job. The job he was trained for. Then he saw a dark figure stand up, head wrapped in a black cloth. The figure was waving, beckoning.

What he understood of the world, the bad guys were
the ones in black turbans. "Go join your brother," he said to
himself. His finger squeezed gently on the trigger again.

* * *

Yusuf was cursing continuously. When Abdi had not
come back for the feast he had set out to find him. But he
had been too late. The bitch had turned Abdi. He would lose
a son and a hostage. The guards had met him, drunk, high on
quat and ashamed. They said Abdi and the woman had gone.
He had run for the boats. They were stupid. They had taken
one boat but left the other tied up. He jumped down into the
boat. He would find them. Alone he would be faster. When
he wired up the AIS he smiled. She was stupid. She had
activated the transponder as well as the receiver. She was
sending out a signal, the signal of the ship he had wrenched
the AIS from. Now he could follow them.

He wasn't smiling now. On the AIS he could see
Abdi's skiff. And he could see the American ship ahead of
Abdi. Surely they would know not to head for that? It was
certain death. No-one would head at full speed towards an
American ship. Too many innocent fishermen had died
already doing that.

He thought they had seen sense. He saw Abdi slow
and stop. He would get them. He would punish the woman,
but he would not kill her. She had value. He needed her to
get the rest of the ransom paid. Then Abdi would marry
Amina and he would be back in power.

But then they were moving again towards the
American ship. In the distance he saw a flashing light. Then
the gun flashes. He saw Abdi's boat stop suddenly. He didn't
want to become a second target and he swung the boat in a
wide arc, turning to run. He heard a second long burst of fire.
His back tensed. He thought it was for him.

On the AIS the trace of the *Fanja* suddenly disappeared. Now there was only the American ship on the screen, and it was moving away quickly. The American ship did not change course or speed.

There was nothing he could do. He had lost a valuable hostage. He had lost a son. But he still held a ship and he could still get money. Yusuf settled the throttle to a steady cruise and held his head while the boat took him home.

* * *

There would not be another raid today. There would be no wedding for Amina. Yusuf thought that if there was no wedding he had less need for cash. He was back at the ship. The guards kept well clear of him. He was glad not to have to go to sea again immediately.

Out of the afternoon sun the small plane flew slowly towards them. His mobile phone was alive with calls. Here was the last of the money. He would pay off the boys and release the ship.

The bright orange packet landed squarely on the deck. Within minutes he was handing bundles of notes to the boys. There was no arguing. No-one would argue with Yusuf today. They took the cash, thumbed through the bundles quickly, then stashed them carefully into belts close to their skin. They were ready to go ashore, ready to go home. Go home rich, which made them targets.

The hunters were now the hunted. They had extorted the cash from the shipowners. Now they had to run the gauntlet of militias and bandits to get their share of the cash to safety. Too many people would have seen the plane dropping the cash. They were nervous, checking their guns and looking around. They wanted to be moving before it got dark.

Finally Yusuf was done. "Captain," he called. The old man walked slowly across the deck from where he stood with the crew. They were watching, fascinated by the piles of cash disappearing into pockets and inside loose robes. "Captain," said Yusuf expansively. "The ship is yours. We go house now. When you see our boat reach shore you call office. You move ship, go away, go Al Shabab, go where you like. We listen. You call too soon, we come back, kill you. Understand?"

The captain nodded. Suddenly the pirates began shaking hands with all the crew. They were laughing, happy. It was like a leaving party between two crews. Could they keep in touch? Send me an email when you get home? I come Germany to meet you, yes? The crew did not know how to respond.

Yusuf led the pirates into the skiff. It was heavily loaded with the whole guard. It took twenty minutes for them to reach the shore. The captain watched them go through the surf. Then he turned to look at the crew.

"OK," he said simply. "Let's go."

CHAPTER THIRTY-ONE

Yusuf felt good. He looked around the courtyard of his Ristorante. To his right the self-elected minister of fisheries was chewing fresh green new quat shoots. A large supply had been flown in from Kenya that day. To his left a group of clan elders were picking over the quat while vying for his attention. To have money was good. It made people behave.

He thought he would call Ah Hing later. Fix a delivery for more boats and motors. More fuel. Some more weapons. Word had spread that his boys had been paid. Others were dropping by now, hungry young men with guns, asking when the next trip would be. "*Inshallah*, if the weather is good, we will patrol for a ship next week," said Yusuf. He waved them all into the yard, there was quat for all of them. Another ship would be easy money, he thought. I can relax and send these others. The restaurant will be back in business and the politicians will come here only for cash and quat.

He snapped his fingers for a servant. He wanted whisky. As she approached he looked up and caught a glimpse of Amina. She was in the doorway, looking at him. She was shrouded in black but he could see her red eyes.

Crying again, he thought. What use to cry, the boy is dead, there will be another boy. He waved her away, back out of sight. For a moment his good mood faltered. His wife was sad, his daughter crying. He had to call Ahmed. He would have to explain that Abdi was dead. That there would be no wedding.

He could do that tomorrow. He forgot about Amina and Ahmed and Abdi. Today was for success. Today was for power. Today was for being generous with cash and quat. "Black Label," he said loudly, "it goes well with quat. The Coastguard is working well." He laughed out loud, and he saw that his guests laughed with him.

* * *

John C switched into Greek. "Captain," he said. "I am so glad to hear from you. So happy you are safe and free. I'm sure you knew you could rely on us to look after you. It was always a matter of *philotimo* for us."

The captain was not as polite as he usually was. He supposed he was a little stressed. John C could not quite see why. He had had a nice sunshine holiday for a couple of months and now he was on his way. Wages paid for doing nothing. What was wrong with the man?

"Captain," he said. "There is a change of plan. Vexol has resold the cargo to Kenyan interests. You will take the ship to Mombasa. How long will that take?"

John C was thinking quickly. He had not realised that it was so close.

"Captain," he replied. "It is probably important not to go full speed so soon after such a long anchorage. Try to get to Mombasa not before the day after tomorrow. I need to make proper arrangements for the reception of you and your crew. Is that clear?"

He dialled again, reaching Ellis after one ring. That boy is just too keen, he thought. He jumped at the order to get some security in place in Mombasa to stop the crew leaving the ship or talking to anyone on arrival. He seemed to relish the idea of flying out to Mombasa and meeting the ship. John C thought he could rely on him to make the crew understand their options.

He read Ellis' mind. He would have done the same himself. "Of course," he replied, in a man to man tone. "Of course you will have to take an assistant, Ellis. You'll need help with taking the statements and getting the confidentiality agreements signed. I don't want anyone stepping off that ship until they are quite clear that they will say nothing about this to anyone, or they will never work again."

He put the phone down. He wondered which of the pretty young assistant lawyers in Ellis' office would be offered the chance of a trip to Kenya.

John C scrolled through the clippings he had received from his PR people. Lloyd's List, Tradewinds, Fairplay, great, he was on Reuters and Bloomberg. Why couldn't they get the FT? He would have liked more but it was still good. That was a great statement, some great headlines. "CanDo frees crew safely", "Canopoulos say Can Do attitude important when dealing with pirates", "Leading owner pans piracy protection", they had got the main points. His ship was free because he had acted. The navies were failing but owners were looking after themselves. The crews were what mattered and money was secondary.

He thought he might keep the ship. It was useful to be a shipowner. He would see if he could join some industry task forces on piracy. Make a public fuss on behalf of INTERTANKO or the International Chamber of Shipping or some other bunch of busybodies. Then when his wife coughed up and CanDoCars started pumping money, who knows, he thought. With a high and caring public profile like that anything was possible. A knighthood, perhaps?

He sat back. He just needed to hear from Ellis now that the confidentiality agreements had been signed and the crew dispersed to their homes. It was a pity about that Norwegian girl, he had not even realised there was a girl on the ship. Why the hell had he been employing a girl seafarer, he thought. I'll speak to the operations manager, he should have guessed having a girl on board would lead to complications. Good job she was Norwegian anyway, he thought. No-one outside Norway will remember her for long.

He looked at his watch. What time was it in Kenya? Bloody Ellis had better be getting on with the job, he thought. If he wants to get inside the knickers of some posh totty would-be lawyer, that had to come after getting the job done.

CHAPTER THIRTY-TWO

Diana had looked great in that thin blouse last night, thought Ellis. A session in the pool and a good dinner tonight might just persuade her to take it off. She must be impressed. Business class flights, all expenses at the Mombasa Serena Beach Hotel. Juniors should jump for a chance of a trip like this. Just get this job done and they could get back to the pool. I bet she looks great in a bikini, he thought.

Ellis glanced up at Diana. She was sitting across the table from him in the captain's office on the *Prometheus*. She looks pale, thought Ellis. Damn ship is a bit of a mess. The crew have had nothing to do for months, you'd think they could keep it clean.

"Captain," he began, slowly and clearly in his speaking-to-foreigners voice. "We can do this easily and quickly as long as the crew understand their best interests. I rely on you to help them understand that."

The captain was not showing any emotion. Another old cuddy, thought Ellis. Too old for this sort of thing, he should be at home on his grotty little island, cuddling some granny in a black dress. "It is very straightforward. I have prepared a statement for you and for each of the crew. It sets out exactly the precautions you took to avoid capture by pirates and explains that you have been held in good conditions since your precautions failed. It notes your gratitude to the owner for ensuring your safety and for ransoming the ship quickly. Separately Diana has a confidentiality agreement and an indemnity agreement for you and for each crew member. You and they will sign to agree that you will never speak about this period and will release CanDoTank from any form of liability as a result of your failure to defend yourselves against the pirates."

He stopped. The captain was impassive, looking at him without moving. What was wrong with the old fool? Perhaps his English wasn't so good, thought Ellis.

"Look," he said. "You just sign here and here and you can go home. The owner will pay you up to today even though you have not been working. The crew must follow your example, then they can go home too."

The captain smiled. "And if they don't sign, Mr Ellis? Shall I then point to those big security men who are keeping us prisoner on board the ship since we arrived in port?"

In the sudden silence Diana caught her breath. She seemed upset. Then the captain laughed cynically. "We know how shipowners work, Mr Ellis," he said. "We are not stupid. We want to work again in the future. Pass me the papers. The crew are waiting to sign theirs in the mess room. You can tell Mr Canopoulos that the captain and crew go home quietly."

Great, thought Ellis. Thought the old boy would make trouble for a second then. Loads of time for a snifter by the pool now. It's so hot on this bloody ship but it will be lovely on the sunbeds.

* * *

The rain was drilling the pavements, falling in heavy drops that bounced in small fountains. Their shoes were soaked and the small umbrellas did not keep much of the rain off their robes. They walked slowly on the broken flagstones. Ahead of them the red brick of Butetown Mosque was streaming water. In the gloom of the rain the heavy grey wire protection on the windows gave the mosque a sinister military air.

Ahmed was aware of others, couples and small groups. Some youths. They were all in Somali national dress. They moved slowly towards the mosque. Beside him Nadifa was shaking. From the cold, or grief, Ahmed did not know. He did not know how to talk with Nadifa about Abdi's death.

In his pocket he could feel the letter. It had come that morning. Postmarked Cardiff University. For his son. A place to study optometry. A passport to a different world. It was like a second stab in the heart. He had sent his son to Somalia. To the old world. And he would not come back.

* * *

The rain had reached the west coast of Norway. It had lost heart as it crossed Britain but regained strength as it drove over the North Sea. It was hitting the roof hard enough now to disturb the solid quiet in the plain Lutheran church in Ulsteinvik.

They were all there. The neighbours. The family. Some who had come in suits the night before from Oslo. But Sven and Torild sat alone on the simple pine pew at the front.

Sven could not hear the priest. He did not want to hear him. There was no comfort to come from him. His daughter was dead. Shot by an American ship. Shot only days before the ship was released. Dead, no body to grieve over, and no granddaughter to grow up quiet and tough like her mother.

He had never shown emotion. He would not cry now. Sven sat there staring straight ahead. On the bench, out of sight of the others, he felt Torild's hand touch his.

The End

About the author

John Guy served on merchant ships and warships for sixteen years before becoming a ship inspector and then a journalist. For the last twenty years he has been advising companies and organisations working in the global shipping industry on media and crisis management. This is his first novel.

Previous books by John Guy include:

Marine Surveying & Consultancy

Effective Writing for the Marine Industry

Follow John's blog at www.johnguybooks.com

Read John's second novel, The Golden Tide, published 2014 as a Kindle e-book and as a paperback on Amazon.

The Golden Tide

Green activist Simone struggles with her beliefs when she meets journalist Michiel, who shows her how an oil spill threatening Sicily is a bonanza for many locals. Compensation and clean-up money floods into the community, creating conflicts between politicians, the oil company, environmentalists and locals. Simone and Michiel fight to save the coastline, putting them into a tense and dangerous confrontation with powerful forces which have a different agenda.

Reading Group Discussion Questions

1. How did this book challenge your views on piracy?
2. Why do you think the author chose a British Somali as the main character?
3. Did you enjoy the way the book switched between action in Somalia and behind the scenes in London and Oslo?
4. Were you shocked at the way modern shipping is portrayed?
5. Did the international nature of the book with action in different countries make it richer for you?
6. Think about an eighteen-year old boy you know. Would he have reacted as Abdi did to the circumstances he found himself in?
7. Did the book make you think about the conflicts between upbringing in the UK and links to their parents' mother countries which affect a lot of British youth?
8. Is Lisa a bad woman? What would you have done in her place?
9. The UK government refused to pay a ransom to rescue the British couple Paul and Rachel Chandler when they were kidnapped by Somali pirates from their yacht. Did this book make you change your mind about that decision?
10. Is it right to pay ransoms to pirates to free seafarers?
11. Everything in this book has actually happened in real life. What shocks you most?
12. What most surprised you in the book and why?
13. Piracy affects seafarers in all sorts of places around the globe. Why do you think that we don't hear about it in Europe and the USA?

14. When you buy something it is always made abroad. Do you ever think about how it got to your home country and the people who move goods around the world? Did this book make you think more about what happens at sea?
15. Were you offended by any of the stereotype characters in the book?
16. Was the ending a surprise? Did it satisfy you? Why or why not?

Made in the USA
Lexington, KY
21 January 2014